TO REST OUR MINDS AND BODIES

by Harriet Armstrong

the quick brown fox

Les Fugitives

LONDON

First published in the United Kingdom by Les Fugitives in 2025.
This second edition published in 2026 •
• Les Fugitives Ltd, 91 Cholmley Gardens, Fortune Green Road, London NW6 1UN • www.lesfugitives.com • Cover design by Sarah Schulte and Les Fugitives • Cover artwork 'Floating' 2013 © Yoshitomo Nara, courtesy of the Yoshitomo Nara Foundation • Text design by Juliette Lépineau • All rights reserved • No part of this publication may be reproduced, stored in a retrieval system or transmitted in any form or by any means, electronic, mechanical, photocopying, recording or otherwise, without prior permission in writing from Les Fugitives editions •
A CIP catalogue record for this book is available from the British Library •
• The rights of Harriet Armstrong to be identified as author of this work have been identified in accordance with Section 77 of the Copyright, Designs and Patents Act 1988 •
• Printed in the UK by CMP •

Curating a list of innovative works of literary fiction and narrative non-fiction originally written in English, the quick brown fox collection includes, at the time of print, novels and hybrid texts by Harriet Armstrong, Charlotte Beeston, Penelope Curtis, Lauren Elkin, Olufemi Terry, Erica Van Horn, Kyra Wilder, and Brian Willems.

Praise for *To Rest Our Minds and Bodies*:

'Armstrong is unafraid to look honestly at sex, love and humiliation, and consequently has written a book that is both confronting and warm.' – Rachel Connolly, author of *Lazy City*

'Armstrong [writes] girlhood like a field study – obsessive, precise, and unexpectedly tender.' – Madeline Cash, author of *Earth Angel*

'An astonishingly poised, absorbing debut.' – Alice Blackhurst, author of *Luxury, Sensation and the Moving Image*

'A work of art. Armstrong's prose has that meticulous and urgent quality reminiscent of Beckett and Duras, achieving the same uncanny shared consciousness that keeps you hooked from the first sentence … It cuts through the platitudes of love and life in a way most writers wouldn't dare.' – Luke Kennard, author of *Notes on the Sonnets*

The rarest debut … A must-read, a new immediate classic, a heart-wrenching work of fiction that for once tells the real truth about being young, ravenous, desperate, too big for the container of the body of youth.' – Luke B. Goebel, author of *Fourteen Stories, None of Them Are Yours*

'*To Rest Our Minds and Bodies* is a poignant portrait of the uncertain state of being alive.' – Rebecca Watson, author of *Little Scratch*

'Reading this felt like being given pure, clean glasses after wearing really stressfully and depressingly dirty glasses for many years.'
– Adelaide Faith, author of *Happiness Forever*

'There is something so beautifully gentle, humane and optimistic about the writing, that is uplifting despite the sadness of the plot. This is ultimately unflinching and brave prose.' – SJ Naudé, author of *The Alphabet of Birds*

'A feminist statement of mental unravelling, which is also a plea for the life of the mind ... Armstrong has created a form away from such debasing tropes and genres as "sad girl" lit.' – Catherine Taylor, *Observer*

'It's rare to encounter so purely candid and redolent a portrait of a life.' – Lucy Scholes, *Daily Telegraph*

'At times the novel is unbearably intense, like experiencing the essence of obsession as it's lived in every moment – which is not to say that it isn't also very funny.' – Jude Cook, *Guardian*

'Luminous, unsettling and emotionally honest. Armstrong has captured not how things are, but how they feel.' – Ruby Eastwood, *Irish Times*

'The syntax is unusual and highly specific, punctuated by hundreds of 'somehow's, 'actually's and 'suddenly's, as though the young narrator anticipates an incredulous reader. But the effect is to recreate the way that, at that age, it feels like everything that happens to you is happening for the first time ever.' – Laura Hackett, *The Times*

'Armstrong [shows] the reader the world through the eyes of a somewhat disassociated consciousness now tortured – a kind of adolescence on steroids – and this is deeply absorbing ... The novel aligns with contemporary writing such as *Convenience Store Woman* by Japanese author Sayaka Murata ... The ending of the novel is a tour de force.' – Fiona O'Connor, *Morning Star*

'The story hinges on a first love-come-unrequited romantic experience. This asymmetrical power dynamic, rooted in devotion, sets the novel on a path of relational uncertainty, emotional restraint, and an ongoing tension between mechanical detachment and human vulnerability.' – Brynne Valentine, *Review 31*

'An unflinching testament to the pains of youth.' – Frances Forbes-Carbines, *wonders and wickedness*

TO REST

OUR MINDS

AND

BODIES

I spent the week before my final year began on holiday with my family. Really I was still a child then and sharing a hotel double bed with my child brother. We had so many arguments about the air conditioning, with me desperately wanting it on and him randomly but really persistently wanting it off. It was so revolting to me to feel the sheets clinging to my sweaty skin, I really couldn't take it, it made me feel like some piece of meat or fish being prostrated for sale outside some shopfront lying there sweating like that. I slept so badly that week and had so many stupid dreams, dreams like walking down cold marble steps into an infinite expanse of deep black water I had thought was a floor. At the end of this dream the dream had become self-aware and had given itself a title, which was Floorless, like flawless. My dumb dream thought it was so witty.

On that holiday I learnt to float passively on my back, to suspend my body on water without exerting any effort at all. I spent hours lying on the water's surface squinting up at the sun and feeling myself being carried away from the shore towards nothing. It was the first time I had been swimming since I had become really conscious of ideas like the body and virginity and penetration and so I was hyperaware of the feeling of the water lapping at my body's thresholds, I was wondering the whole time at the back of my mind whether the water might enter me and flow into my core through all those interior channels and passageways. I really did want to know how far inside of me the water might get.

For some reason everything I wore on that holiday was terrible, somehow I had no choice and had to keep wearing all these terrible things. I was wearing some awful pair of water sandals which were a very bright aqua colour and had these densely closed toes, they looked like great blue cockroaches latching themselves onto my feet and digging their claws into my soles. Everyone kept mistaking me for a boy which had never happened before and I didn't understand why it was suddenly happening now, I had long hair and everything although it was maybe a boyish form of long hair, random pieces everywhere with really random lengths. I wasn't sure why my hair had become like that.

That holiday I was obsessed with the idea that I should be reading books as rapidly as possible, somehow gathering all of human experience and great human thought inside of me and storing it away for some time in the future when it would be necessary. It was depressing, sitting there trying to read all these classic books as rapidly as possible, trying to read maybe one classic book a day, reading in the car and getting carsick and having to stare out the window at the sea and the black tarmac of the road as it skidded by beneath me, that endlessly disappearing tarmac and the endlessly present pale sea and my book held tightly in both hands, it was very depressing.

Secretly I couldn't engage with books at all that summer. Books really had nothing to say about the way that life seemed to vomit itself out, some pointless set of images just spewing itself out forever and in front of my eyes and it was impossible to turn it off and impossible to find meaning in it. Meaning and death were both so alienating and that made books inaccessible, but still it was very important to read as I sat there in the car above the tarmac.

I was really feeling, at that time, some need to contextualise myself inside the world, to position myself as a piece of something bigger, something very fundamental. I was creating a kind of self-educational PowerPoint about different foundational concepts, Marxism, Impressionism, I was planning to cover every concept and I felt that when I was finished I would somehow be a part of things, somehow held very tightly by the world and surrounded by things I understood and could master or relate to. I really wanted to make sense in relation to the things that were around me, that was important to me.

○

I felt really indifferent about returning to university. I felt that I knew what university was and it was fine, it was some other location in which life took place. Still to me location felt trivial. Mostly what was thrilling to me was to unpack my things into some new room. It was so satisfying to have a space which was entirely mine and which had to hold my whole life. It was so lovely that my printer had to lie down on the awful brown carpet right next to my ring binder folders and my trainers and boots, right beneath my raincoat. I had always wanted to see all of my possessions at once without moving my face.

The room itself was weird. Everything was wooden and the wood had an artificial-looking orange colour. It was an attic room so all the ceilings were sloped and all the windows were high up on the ceilings and very dirty and showed only the sky. This made the room feel very intimate: I would never have to close my blinds unless I personally and specifically wanted to. There was a huge black beam running through the room which made me think of suicide.

This new room came with a communal windowless bathroom. After I unpacked my things I had a bath in there. I added peach-scented bubble bath which someone had left beside the bath and then regretted it, felt somehow infringed upon by its presence in the water. From the bathroom I could hear somebody playing Don't Stop Believin' on the piano. It felt like the water was moving in response to the piercing notes of Don't Stop Believin'.

○

I was assigned a dissertation project and a supervisor in the Department of Developmental Psychology. My dissertation project turned out to be a sort of basic labour. I had to watch these videos someone had taken of babies sitting on a rag and surrounded by various objects. By looking at each individual frame of each video I had to identify the moments at which the babies first touched the objects, and the moments when they let them go. Then I logged the timings of those moments into a spreadsheet. I really spent hours looking closely at the hands of babies as they moved towards and then away from the material world. There was some suggestion that babies who touched more things might be better at speaking. That was the suggestion we were trying to test.

My dissertation group went for dinner so that we could all meet each other. Everyone in the group was a woman so we had a conversation about being women in academic contexts. People had terrible stories about supervisors asking them out or making lewd comments about their bodies and appearances. I had no stories to share. I didn't understand what it was that shielded me from these sorts of situations, I was grateful of course but it did worry me: was the fact that nothing bad ever happened to me linked with the fact that nothing happened to me at all. Somehow through existing I repelled action.

○

A few days after I returned to university I went to my favourite cafe in the city. The cafe had horrible watery coffee but was full of small cheap treats like tiny soft cookies and it looked out over this field and river. All the walls were glass so it was easy to see everything that was happening there beside that field and river, you could see this man-made waterfall and a long trail of little empty boats and people walking dogs out in the distance and a woman reading a newspaper by the riverbank. Then out of the windows on the other side of the cafe were the tops of houses, I saw two houses joined together by a kind of glass box or passageway, it looked like a greenhouse and really fascinated me, wouldn't the glass break upon contact, break and shatter onto the pavement below as soon as somebody set foot in it. I closed my eyes and imagined the feeling: small shards of glass falling straight from the sky.

○

This year was going to be full of practical classes, classes about very practical things like statistics and computers and human anatomy. In the first statistics class we sat around the corners of a basement and an old man tried to explain the concept of the bell curve. He told us all to hold our breath and count how many seconds we could hold it for. Then we had to write our numbers on the whiteboard so the old man could plot them onto a graph on a separate whiteboard. That graph was supposed to come out shaped like a bell curve. The numbers did actually make a bell curve and mine was the lowest, so low that the old man said it was a statistical outlier. My value was so far from all the others that the old man said we could infer that the person who produced it wasn't trying at all, they weren't taking the activity seriously. This really depressed me. I would drown so easily.

○

I went to the term's first meeting of the literary society. I really hated the literary society but somehow I stayed hopeful, I was still so full of hope for the literary society, I kept feeling that one day I might learn to love that society and really flourish in it. I kept feeling all the time that something might change and open up and I would suddenly become a part of things and really let go in the literary society and bring something great to the table. Sometimes I came prepared to articulate some little theory I had authored, some theory like A lack of narrative structure as a means of expressing the existential meaninglessness of time. I was always so hopeful and drank so much of the red wine that was handed out for free there in foam cups. I was always thinking that the wine might transport me a bit or that it might produce some kind of atmosphere which would be somehow conducive to my self-expression but it had no effect on me at all or on the room, I stayed silent and totally vacant, maybe just marginally more clumsy, maybe I bumped into one or two more chair legs when I had drunk that wine. But on any kind of fundamental level substances really didn't touch me, it was amazing.

In the meeting everyone was talking about Frank O'Hara and at that time I hadn't read any Frank O'Hara. People weren't even discussing his poetry, they were discussing all these aspects of his biography. Some boy in a ragged jumper kept telling an anecdote about how if Frank O'Hara hadn't written poetry he would have died. He kept saying I mean rhetorically of course and another boy kept saying No no he really would have died, you have no idea. I couldn't work out if the whole conversation was a joke. I sank my nails a bit into the yellow skin on the inside of my arm. It was so depressing, that I never had anything to say to anyone. I really had nothing to say about Frank O'Hara's imaginary death or anything else, it was terrible.

But back in my room I did read some Frank O'Hara and discovered that I really loved him. I really admired his nonchalance, I felt that his voice was very optimistic and positive and made distress into something which existed just casually on the side of life but which was not at all overpowering or threatening. After all the terrible things

I do how amazing it is to find forgiveness and love. I thought about that line a lot, so much that the line became my default thought. That week I went for long walks through the city thinking only of this line of Frank O'Hara's. After all the terrible things I do. How amazing it is.

○

I spent a lot of time, in those first days, really just sitting in my room in the dark. It made me feel somehow guilty and even entirely worthless and evil to sit there watching TV or some random movie and sometimes it even made me feel guilty to read a book, what was I contributing to by reading some book in my room, really nothing. Sitting there doing nothing didn't make me feel guilty because it was so unenjoyable, it was horrible just sitting on the floor for some unspecified amount of time with no foreseeable event coming to save me and end that awful period of sitting.

After a few days I started filling some of that time with course readings. There was no end to the number of course readings I could do and as I read I made notes on loose sheets of paper, it was a really material way of signifying progress, that cheered me up. In the second week of term I had to go to WHSmith to buy a new pad of paper and I felt that that was it, that I had made it, that was what success was, having to buy a new pad of paper in only the second week of term. But obviously there was a deeper and more fundamental part of me which course readings couldn't touch at all.

○

Most of my early readings were on anthropology. The course guide had said that anthropology was the study of meaning and that was what I did want to study, meaning, I did very badly want to know what things fundamentally meant. I still felt that everything around me had some hidden core, I felt that the most important and central meanings were concealed and had to be effortfully unearthed. I really couldn't wait for all those meanings to be revealed to me, I would do anything to have all of those meanings revealed.

The first anthropology lecture was on gifts. There was this theory that gifts served the purpose of binding people to each other. If someone gave you a gift then you were bound to them forever, or until you gave them an equivalent gift. If you gave them an equivalent gift then the bond would dissolve and you would be free. This was different to commodities, which were not socially meaningful, and tied nobody to anything.

In our seminar the supervisor Christina asked us if the seminar was a gift or a commodity. I thought this was easy, I said It's a commodity because we pay tuition fees.

Christina looked disparaging and almost actually hateful then and she said I'm not paid enough to be handing out commodities. The implication then was that the seminar was a gift, and that I was bound to Christina for the rest of my life. I felt that one of us had surely misunderstood the concept of the gift completely.

○

That year I had to share public spaces with so many people, my bathroom was shared with six people and my kitchen with eight. This bothered me, I didn't want to get up to go and make breakfast and be faced with some shirtless boy cooking ramen. I felt very visible all the time with all those shared things. All those shared things and the public courtyards which connected them made me think all the time of Foucault's panopticon. I was constantly thinking of Foucault's panopticon, then.

One morning I was cooking porridge and a very tall boy with this golden bob haircut came in and started cooking porridge too, both of us with our little pans on the induction stove. He said Hey and I said Hi and he said I'm Luke and then we had a long extended conversation about how he was a Master's student studying computers and I was a third year doing some vague multidisciplinary social science course. It was a very boring conversation but I was so disappointed when both our pots of porridge finished cooking, I watched Luke leave the kitchen and I wanted to follow him down the hall shouting And tell me what exactly do you learn about computers. It wasn't just because I wanted to prolong the conversation, the fact that Luke was studying computers really did make me think there must be something fascinating about computers which I had all along failed to detect.

I stayed in my room for the whole rest of that day, sitting by the window on my laptop. I spent a long time looking through Luke's Facebook account and I discovered that he was very popular. There were so many photos of him on Facebook, pages and pages of photos, and he was having a good time in almost all of them, at the pub or in someone's well decorated and darkly lit room. He had a very serious face in lots of the photos, he just stared at the person taking the photo very passively without expression. He looked very handsome when he did that passive face, he looked strikingly similar to Tilda Swinton. In my favourite photo Luke had eyeshadow on and was doing a quiet half-smile and standing with his arm around a person who was, I guessed, his girlfriend.

○

I went to an event where you could talk about neurodiversity with different people in the university who were supposed to help you with your problems. This was an activity I was somehow owed because of having dyspraxia and I felt bad about this, I felt that I would be really wasting someone's time sitting down with them and talking about dyspraxia. It felt like sitting down and talking about how I might knock over a glass of water by accident sometimes, I didn't see how I had earned that at all. I was already feeling in some vague and unarticulated way that I had no access to the things I needed, and some excessive kind of access to the things I didn't need at all, and didn't deserve. Still, though, it seemed right: to pursue help.

The event happened inside a conference centre, and had trays of little sandwiches and tropical fruit slices lying around on the conference tables. No one mentioned all this food, it wasn't for us. I sat down and then people walked around and helped me with my time management. They passed round giant sheets of paper which listed every day within October, and you could write your schedule and commitments on the page, using a biro. Somehow I ended up planning out my month in a huge amount of detail and writing in all the different times in which I would work on my readings and essays on the giant sheet, I spent almost an hour doing that and at the end I didn't really want that random schedule, I felt really guilty about that, about the whole thing. I hoped that by the next workshop I might have some more material problems to discuss, some commitments to reschedule, something new to plan for.

○

My friend Anna came back to university and we went for a walk along the river and discussed our summers. Anna had spent most of the summer in Spain with her family and now she was navigating a situation where her friend Grace accused her of being too emotionless in arguments. It wasn't that Anna was unkind, Grace just thought she seemed unmoved somehow, too passive and disinterested. This was the sort of situation I could talk about endlessly, I loved complex but ultimately arbitrary emotional dilemmas. It was linked, too, with this robot joke me and Anna were always making, the joke was that we both felt like robots, like we were acting on our environments robotically, without real emotion or any kind of organic desire to engage. Me and Anna talked about the robot thing a lot. Sometimes we would see some appliance, some kettle or TV in the common room or an old discarded lighter on the street, and we would say Oh look, another robot. Occasionally Anna would stop and say Hello robot! That always killed me, that Hello robot extension of the robot joke.

○

Anna and I were both taking a course on language and the first class was very disappointing to us. We had thought the course would address language in the broadest sense, that it would break open our social relationships and senses of self and in breaking them open illuminate some great singular truth about connection and communication, really about life itself and love and meaning, but instead the class was about some process where babies' throats change as they age. It turned out that as babies got older, their throats got tighter. This was because it was easier for babies to speak when they had a more tight throat. For some reason though it wouldn't have worked if babies had been born with that tight throat, that tightness had to develop progressively and very gradually. Anna and I kicked each other under the table as we listened to these descriptions of the babies' increasingly tight throats. On the way back to our rooms we bought a giant packet of custard creams to share because the lecture hadn't made us feel good at all.

It was hard to know what it was that I wanted to learn. I wanted to learn something that would shock me, something that came from someplace very far outside of myself. I was tired of learning things I could have pulled out of my own mind very easily and passively. It was really hard to think of things that might shock me like that, it was hard to think of things that were outside myself.

That evening I went into the kitchen to cook some pad thai ready meal which was made up of lots of little packets of ingredients which had to be heated separately and then combined in a huge pan, it was a really inefficient ready meal. Luke was in there too, frying tiny pieces of aubergine. Luke was acting like a model of an approachable, delightful person, he was acting like an actor placed inside my kitchen to delight me. He had created an impression of a heartbeat where he kicked the loose wooden board beneath the stove so that the board vibrated and made this great alarming thudding noise. I had never met anyone who would do something like that, who would just stand around the kitchen very casually and freely showing some random girl a heartbeat impression on the clapboard. The noise didn't especially remind me of a heartbeat but it was an evocative sound for sure and I was so charmed by how hilarious Luke found his own heartbeat impression, he really was adamant that I kept watching as he kicked the board again and again, and again and again made that great thudding sound, and somehow it did become hilarious, all that thudding, all those fake stupid heartbeats. In the background of the heartbeats I could hear Luke's music, some genre of pop music I had never heard before, some hysterical breathy pop music that made me feel anxious at first and then this new thing, I wasn't sure what it even was, what I should call it.

○

I started going into the kitchen when I thought I could hear Luke in there. The kitchen was right next to my room and my room's walls were very thin so this quickly became a very consuming project. Sometimes I actually heard Luke's voice but mostly it was the vague echoes of music that I heard, or even just footsteps or the opening and closing of doors which I for some reason linked with the concept of his presence. Often I was wrong, it wasn't Luke but someone else, and I would have to perform some action which would both explain my presence in the kitchen and legitimise my immediate departure. I would turn the kettle on, for example, or take someone's random orange to my room, and then sit at my desk, totally deflated, sometimes for half an hour, even longer.

But then sometimes it would be Luke. We would both grin and say Oh, hi with almost sarcastic delight, and lay our ingredients out on the counters, set our pans down on the stove. One evening Luke told me about his dissertation project, designing virtual reality models of real-life objects: trainers, doorways, wheels. He said that his friend Callum was making a robot which could categorise personality based on five traits: agreeableness, openness, conscientiousness, extraversion and neuroticism. I told Luke I had none of those positive traits but high levels of neuroticism i.e. a bad personality and he laughed a lot. As he laughed he passed me a teaspoon of his curry and I couldn't even taste the curry because I was thinking about how his fingers had touched each piece of onion, each piece of potato, some of the lentils, some of the mustard seeds, all of these things which were now inside my mouth, and I said, Oh, it's amazing.

○

The lectures on the gift went on, they kept happening. I sat in some lecture hall on Thursday morning and watched a film called *Ongka's Big Moka*. A man called Ongka was preparing a great moka – moka was gift – and the moka was so great that preparing it was completely ruining him and his tribe. It really seemed that preparing the moka would cause his tribe's permanent downfall, it was something they would never recover from. The moka included so many vehicles and animals and also tens of thousands of dollars, it wasn't surprising that his tribe couldn't afford all these things. But somehow Ongka felt that through creating the moka he would win back everything he had lost in preparing it, the moka would be so impressive as to be completely defeating and it would make all of the suffering worthwhile.

At the end of the film Ongka succeeded, and he said to the moka's recipient: Now that I have given you these things, I have won. I have knocked you down by giving so much. Most of the film was really difficult to follow, Ongka's tribe kept talking and so did some man giving a kind of booming narration, none of the voices were audible, but I understood Ongka's final words very clearly. I have knocked you down by giving so much.

○

Suddenly then there was a lot of work to do, I had to answer so many questions about the bell curve and statistics and to write an essay on the moka. I did these things in the arts and humanities campus of the university, this great square of grass and concrete surrounded by so many different libraries. There was even a cafe there, it was a very encompassing environment. I actually loved those days I spent just working on that campus. It really made me feel free, to wake up and walk to the campus and spend the day moving between the different libraries there and doing different tasks that had been assigned to me. Somehow that felt like freedom to me, sitting there doing all the different tasks I had been told to do by people who were older than me and who were able to really evaluate me. That was very compelling, that impending evaluation.

○

I went for coffee with my friend Héloise. We sat in a cafe full of silent people on laptops and she told me about a new routine she had started for final year. Héloise went to this cafe every morning and read articles from the *Guardian* on her iPad. Then she went for a one-hour run through fields. Then she had a bath. Then her day could begin. Conversations like this always depressed me, I was always assuming that everyone was the same and had the same depressing lack of initiative and spontaneous thought but no, it was particularly me who lacked these things. I would never go for a one-hour run through fields, I would never even read the *Guardian*, I would just never think to do these things.

Héloise told me about a hike she had been on over the summer, she had been on a great hike through mountains and had met a man she really liked, and had slept with him. He had a girlfriend in Italy, he was from Italy too and had gone back there now forever. Still they were staying in touch, just two days ago he had sent her a photo of the view from his apartment, a red sun hung over mountains. There were so many mountains in this anecdote, mountains from all these different parts of the world coming together in the story of this man and his Italian girlfriend. Héloise said that she was worried she should stop talking to the man, she was worried she was letting men strip her of her sense of self again. When she said this I nodded like I knew what it was like to have my sense of self stripped away from me by men, like I was sitting there right at that moment watching my sense of self being really dragged away from me. There it goes, my sense of self.

○

When I got back to my room I tried to open up my body, like I did whenever anyone reminded me of sex: that it existed, people did it, people did it all the time. I used my fingers to try and find the gap but the whole area was tightly shut. I tried using the dull end of a pencil but the pencil couldn't find a way in and dropped to the ground. Google told me the problem had lots of different causes. Maybe I had a problem with my mental health or self-esteem, maybe I was scared of feeling pain, maybe I thought sex was shameful. Maybe I thought sex was evil. But I didn't know how to work out whether or not I thought that sex was evil, and whether or not I hated myself and had depression. I thought of Luke, stirring his food inside the kitchen with his body leant against the wall, his back against the wall so that he faced the stove side-on as he faced me. Would he be able to reach inside me with his body if he tried to, would he know how he was meant to use his hands and mouth and muscles to get into me and reach the inner heart? I cut that florid, stupid thought out of my internal monologue and put the pencil in the bin.

On Friday I accidentally walked into the kitchen while Luke and his girlfriend were cooking together. Luke's girlfriend was wearing a dressing gown but then also lipstick and had some kind of pattern on her nails which was lots of swirling lines intersecting with each other. She said Hi I'm Mia and I realised there was music coming from my phone and Mia said about the music Is this Mitski and I said Yeah. I took two falafel balls from the fridge then and put them on a plate and left without acknowledging Luke at all. I really left just carrying that horrible plate of cold and actually wet falafel balls which weren't even mine, a cold plate of some random person's wet falafel balls.

In my room I tried to keep distracting myself by brushing my teeth until my tongue and cheeks were stinging and covered in tiny red bumps. I was listening to Mitski really loudly, so loudly that Mia could maybe hear it from the kitchen. Mia and Luke might have been kissing to the Mitski they could hear through the wall. Mitski heard through a brick wall, that must be a romantic sound.

It snowed that night, it really snowed in October and I woke up the next morning with snow covering my windows because they were slanted skylight windows which the snow could actually settle on and eclipse completely. When I opened my blinds it was as if I hadn't opened them at all, the snow was a second and unopenable blind behind them and the room stayed dark. I walked to the botanic gardens and looked at the plants all covered over with snow, all of those snow-covered plants just lying there indistinguishable and yet retaining their endless separate Latin names flaunted on endless little placards. The names really did nothing, it was obvious that the plants were all the same, that they were stupid impotent things unable to dig themselves out or to uncover themselves at all.

There was a lake in the centre of the botanic gardens but it wasn't frozen over. When I got back to my room the windows were clear again.

○

I went to an incomprehensible lecture about vision. The lecturer was trying to explain how our perceptions of objects are transferred through so many differently named sections of the eye: the cornea, the macula, the limbus, the vitreous body. Visions went through each part of the eye to the part behind it and then were reflected to some other part and transmitted to a fourth part and went through that part to another part, just pinging between these parts forever. The separations between all the obviously connected parts of the eye seemed distracting and completely extraneous to the production of knowledge and yet somehow they formed the whole body of the lecture, so that learning about vision became learning lists of pseudowords and their designated orders. It made all knowledge feel invented, like in the theory that the eye was made by God because it was too complex to have been made by evolution.

I started thinking about Luke's virtual objects as I sat there beneath the barred windows of the lecture hall. I wondered if our eyes would see his objects differently, if they would know that they were flat impersonations of the world made inside of a computer, or if they would be tricked and send signals to our body shouting Look so that our fingers would reach out to touch something, some shoe or doorway, and be met with nothing, our eyes and bodies totally out of sync, totally alienated.

○

That evening I sat in some windowless IT room and started writing a story about the gift. The gift was really a metaphor for something unspecific, something vague and diffuse, but a woman died for it, she died because of this great gift she had been given. It was a gift that she could never repay and the person who had given her the gift didn't even want her repayment, they had wanted to give her something priceless and to see her devastating and actually destructive inability to repay it. That was my idea for the story but it was really hard to make it convincing or meaningful without having a clear idea of what the gift was. Any attempt to define the gift made the whole story seem trite, I didn't want to write some dumb story about 'love' for example or some person's sexual awakening and it didn't seem like there was really anything else the gift could be. I walked back from the IT room to my room and my room was just as dark as the stupid IT room had been. Every room was so dark regardless of whether or not it had proper windows.

○

Anna and I were set our first coursework assignment for the language paper. The assignment was to write a two-thousand-word essay on our experiences with language. For example, we could write about our experiences of bilingualism or our experiences of dyslexia, or we could write about our experience of having Specific Language Disorder. There was objectively nothing for me to write my coursework about. I had had no experiences with language, really none. I had never experienced language. In the end I wrote about how I had learnt to read. I learnt to read by being taught to read by teachers. I wrote, in my essay, about the *Biff and Chip* books. I wrote the sentence I progressed through the *Biff and Chip* book series written by Anne-Marie Young and R. Hunt towards increasingly advanced *Biff and Chip* books. It was a terrible essay, no one enjoyed it. Anna wrote about being bilingual in Spanish, she thought it was a stupid essay too but it wasn't at all. Anna's essay was meaningful, relevant and interesting. The only good thing you could say about my essay was that it was true.

○

In the kitchen that night Luke was making some terrible meal, a piece of ham on a microwavable potato waffle. I said I thought you were vegetarian and then I said Why are you eating that. Whenever I had seen Luke in the kitchen before he had been making a really lavish feast, something with fifteen ingredients, something like six separate little salads with totally non-overlapping ingredient sets. Luke said loudly and weirdly as if he was pushing something out of himself Mia broke up with me. I almost took his hand then but instead I said Do you want to have dinner. My heart was beating almost audibly, I could feel its beat inside my arms and chest, it seemed like they were throbbing, hot with blood. Because really I felt very lucky in that moment, I felt absolutely blessed and like my life was finally about to start unfolding and revealing some beautiful core which had been promised to me all along and which was finally here: here it was, the start of life.

We ate in Luke's room. It felt almost illegal to be inside his room, it was so intimate. There were plants everywhere, hanging off the shelves and off the suicide beam I also had in my room. Luke had turned off the overhead light and lit the room with only his bedside lamp and the weak light attached to the sink so that everything was hard to see in any normal level of detail, everything looked vague and gold but at the same time clearly foregrounded and emphasised. All the edges in that room were gilded, the edges of Luke's face, the fine edges of his cheekbones. Luke sat down in his desk chair and I sat in the plush 'lounge' chair with the low coffee table in between us, Luke's little fern resting there in the table's centre, all its felted leaves curled inwards.

I asked him questions about what happened with Mia and he cried a lot and said Thank you so many times and answered all my questions with very long and incoherent answers. He gave off the atmosphere of someone being assaulted by memories and unable to fight them off. The memories he told me didn't tell any kind of story: he was remembering the time when he had sex with Mia on the roof of a library, the time when they had bleached each other's hair, when he developed some kind of skin infection on their holiday to multiple south-eastern French villages. Luke kept saying I was no one before Mia, I was no one before her and then telling me some other memory, some other detail of him and Mia's intimacy, that was the rhythm of the conversation: all those directionless memories and the idea of Luke as no one in the time before them. All those timeframes were activated at once there in Luke's room, the time before and the time during and then this undefined and frightening time after. It did seem very awful when he described it like that.

I realised as I sat there facing Luke that all my life I had assumed, in some unconscious way, that truly overwhelming emotion was false, that it was some person's false invented category, some false construct like femininity or borders or like the specific layout of a particular city or the random tastes which were supposed to be found inside some wine. I had spent my life believing that emotions were the products of cerebral meta-narratives people constructed about their lives, a means of fabricating meaning and elevating life to a more human or more noble level. But here it was, true devastation, and it had nothing to do with meaning or narrative. Here I was with Luke, observing some great breakdown of internal boundaries, some dissolution of the self. Here I was, with Luke curled up in his desk chair opposite me, his face lit up so warmly and so softly in the sink light as he looked me in the eyes and spoke of the deep burning inside of him.

Being in my room acquired a new quality that week. It was partly material. I was treating the light in my room differently, I was really limiting the light in some warm dappled way like Luke had done, keeping that sink light on constantly and the bedside lamp also. I was listening, too, to so much of Luke's music, so many women breathing loudly and anxiously, so many women wailing. I kept listening to a song called Door, this woman singing You open the door to another door to another door in a clear startling voice, that Door song really spoke to me and I did feel that there was a door to another door opening as I sat there in my room in the dim light. I felt that even as I was sitting at my desk and watching dissertation videos. It felt very heavy and very meaningful to watch all of those babies touching objects, all of those babies picking up cups and little cars and setting them down on the carpet. That felt endlessly rich to me suddenly: all those babies, all those touches.

Me and Anna went to a club that week with Anna's boyfriend Jacob and some friend he had and some girl Maddy who was someone's friend also and then someone called Ben. I actually preferred clubbing in stupid incoherent groups like this, it was impossible for me to find clubbing a social experience, it was so physical to feel music beat across my body, to feel music as if it was a kind of heartbeat rather than something I was hearing. I couldn't feel that beating and also engage with anything, that feeling really trapped me inside myself.

I loved that night, I loved moving my body in a vague unconscious way and watching Anna and Jacob dance with each other, a sarcastic sort of dance as if they were dancing together but also mocking the idea that they might be dancing together. No one remembered I was there, I left unnoticed and that was very thrilling to me, walking alone back to my room, walking alone over the river in some weather-inappropriate cropped vest feeling the wind so acutely on my arms. I felt like a kind of angel or ghost somehow, I felt so ethereal right then and so untouchable. My arms looked very white and alien in the moonlight like that, they didn't even look like mine as I noticed them by my sides while I walked along the bridge. Suddenly my arms really looked so different, like the pale arms of some tall girl. It wasn't a bad feeling at all, seeing my arms in that strange way.

○

I messaged Luke the next day asking how he was and he didn't even reply to the question, he just said Shall we go for a drink? Then three hours later we met at a pub. Plans were so easy to make, it was almost alarming how easily I could just meet up with Luke, I really could make anything happen by just typing some words into my phone. I didn't know how I would ever make myself stop, it felt like I would just keep making things happen through my phone forever. I had never felt that way before, like I held within my own specific self the capacity to really make things happen. I had never felt that way before.

Luke and I arrived at the pub separately and then walked through its whole interior together, we walked to the outside section of the pub which stood overlooking the river. We sat down at a two-person table underneath so many glowing heat lamps that we both took off all our jackets and coats and were left in thin T-shirts, Luke's white, mine black and with a strange high neckline. I couldn't stop looking at his face lit up in the warm lighting of the lamps, Luke's face against the slowly moving water behind him and I realised with delight that this was appropriate, that we were actually here to look at each other's faces and listen to each other's voices as they rose up over the hum of the traffic and the faint crashing of the waterfall at the head of the river. This was the gift I had been given, two hours, even more, in which to fill my senses with these things. I thought of Frank O'Hara, of the marvellous experience which was not going to go wasted on him. I look at you and I would rather look at you than all the portraits in the world.

Luke and I spoke about how difficult it could be to speak, to moderate the sound of one's voice, to choose the right moments, find the words to use, the words which would open something up entirely, illuminate it and welcome others in, and how difficult it was to find the will to do these things, to want to prostrate oneself like that at all. It was really shocking to me, that Luke felt this way. I told him this, I said I thought you were immune and he said No, I am definitely worse than you.

We ordered two more beers then through Luke's phone, two pale beers called Lighthouse. Luke started telling me about a dream he had had in which Mia was walking towards him on a thin wooden beam. He was standing in his childhood bedroom and Mia was walking on a suspended wooden beam over his garden. They made eye contact then as she stood there and both their eyes were filled with tears. I said the dream sounded really upsetting and I think I winced a bit, because I meant that completely, it sounded terrible. Already it was unbearable to me, even with Luke sitting opposite me as almost a stranger, the thought of him disappearing from my life and then returning in some stupid dream which existed entirely in my mind, without the real Luke having any idea that I had seen him crying on a wooden beam outside my window as I, too, had cried. That thought made me really depressed.

Luke asked me, then, if I had loved someone, and I suddenly saw myself standing at a frightening crossroads in my life, passing from one frightening chapter into the next, hanging over some great chasm. I said I was a virgin and that I didn't even know what my sexuality was, which felt like the answers to two easier but also plausible questions. Luke said that he wasn't sure either, that he thought he was probably bi but mostly he pictured himself being with girls, and I wanted to say No, no, that isn't what I meant at all, what I meant is that my whole body is on fire and I am very afraid. It had nothing to do with gender. Luke looked at my face then and he said Be kind to yourself, and in that moment this response made more sense than anything I had ever heard and I said I will, I will, the water lapping darkly at the ground beneath our chairs.

On the way back to our rooms we passed a tennis ball lying in the gutter and stood, for some reason, tossing the tennis ball to one another in the middle of the road. I could hear somebody's automatic hosepipes hissing, somebody's moonlit garden being drenched in water.

○

The next morning I woke up early and walked across a square of grass between the road and the river as the sun was rising. There was no one else around and I saw a rat run from the grass into the riverbed. It didn't disgust me at all, I felt a warm rush of communion with that rat as I watched it jump out of sight into the mud. I imagined its paws sinking in, and the relief of that, the relief of being caught as one is falling, caught by something porous and giving, sinking into that thing and looking upwards at the height from which one fell with disbelief. I really did like that little rat as I saw it jump away from me into the river.

    I walked to a cafe then, I thought I would write part of my essay on language acquisition there and I ordered a cappuccino and a piece of some wet-looking carrot cake. The walls of the cafe were covered in quotations that were meant to be hilarious, quotations like It's always wine o'clock even though the cafe didn't sell wine or any alcohol. The woman who made my coffee told me that her name was Seda which meant Echo and I didn't even tell her my name, I just said Your name is beautiful and I really did mean that, I loved that name and the things that it meant, some echo endlessly bouncing between mountains somewhere, leaping from one thing to another without dying, without being lost at all.

○

Suddenly it was so much warmer and when I saw Héloise she made some comment about climate change; this really annoyed me, couldn't we just enjoy nice things.

I became really interested in going outside wearing just T-shirts, somehow it felt like the first time in my life I'd walked around without a coat or jacket and felt the air on my bare skin. That feeling actually felt new to me. That week I went for about a million walks, about a million walks through random parks and fields, suddenly it was very engaging to just experience senses and to listen to Luke's music through headphones, and then to take the headphones off and be so surprised and shocked by how loud the park was, how loud the wind was or some birds or even insects. I would listen to the loudness of those things for a few seconds, maybe a minute, and then I would put the headphones back on and be drowned, again, inside Luke's music, inside a woman's anxious voice of love, all of those endlessly opening doors.

One night I went for a walk outside the libraries and lecture halls, very modern library and lecture hall buildings which really looked beautiful in the dark like that and so majestic, all those glass buildings towering above me. I felt as if I was drunk or as if I was inside some movie looking up at all those buildings in the dark. I was surrounded, suddenly, by large and powerful things, and I felt that those things would hold me. That was really how it felt, that night.

○

I started having a new genre of dream, the dream was just a bunch of objects drifting in front of my eyes. Usually they would be things like pans or kettles or sometimes they would be animals, a fox sitting in a fixed position, a static lizard. In the dream I knew these things were fake, that they formed a sort of catalogue produced for me specifically. My nights would be full of these fake things and then I would wake up to reality and that would be delightful to me, stepping out into that reality each morning.

I loved getting dressed after those dreams, I loved just standing in front of the mirror and watching myself getting ready for the day. On the way back from a statistics class I bought some eyeliner from Boots to put on in front of that mirror and when I put it on I couldn't believe I wasn't already someone who wore loads of random eyeliner all over my face, it was exactly the sort of thing I would do. It really was mesmerising, standing there in front of the mirror and just drawing on my face with some piece of black pencil. Somehow that was an acceptable thing to be doing.

○

Suddenly Luke and I were seeing each other all the time, almost every day we saw each other in the kitchen or had dinner or went to the pub. One night Luke said Sorry am I being too clingy, and I laughed a lot and said No no

Luke you are not. It was wonderful to me, that he felt he was somehow imposing himself upon me when in reality it was obviously me who needed him, it was me who would die if we didn't see each other every day, me who would stand outside his door shouting and shouting and throwing things at the door until he came out. Somehow Luke didn't realise that. That was some great gift, that blindness, I was very grateful for it.

And yet it wasn't at all shocking that he wanted to spend so much time together, it was obvious that being together was completely exhilarating to both of us. It seemed to me that until meeting Luke I had been contracting some muscle or pressing something made of hard impenetrable material very effortlessly during every conversation, I had never really breathed while speaking or even listening before. Suddenly I dreaded neither listening nor speaking, I really longed for both, I welcomed both right into the heart of myself and nothing was contracting at all, everything was wide open and streaming. I felt that if I was any more relaxed then I would fall right into Luke and be unable to get up again, I would be lying right inside him barely needing to breathe.

○

Luke started knocking on my door to lend me clothes. This was so delightful to me and especially delightful because it was such an unnatural thing to do: I would never go and knock on some friend's door with a sweater or jacket I thought they might like to borrow, no one would do that, as an act it lived outside any known systems of meaning.

The first thing Luke lent me was a huge and ancient-seeming sweater. I felt so immune when I wore this sweater, I felt totally untouchable and sat on the top floor of the library with my hands buried in its long and heavy sleeves. Sometimes I would throw my head back slightly with real delight at the smell of this sweater which I was allowed to wear on my own body, this sweater which tied me to Luke, which tied me to him forever or until I returned the sweater to him.

On another morning he lent me a huge leather coat. As I was walking to the library in this huge coat I walked past Mia and almost made some small vomit in my mouth, I had to regulate my breathing for a long time after that. It was just so shocking to me on a really visceral level, to remember that Mia was real, that Luke and I existed in the world and were surrounded by people who could see us and who even knew us. I had almost forgotten that Mia wasn't a person Luke had invented. Mostly what I felt, though, was excitement, intense and even nauseating excitement at the idea of Mia seeing me in Luke's old coat and wondering what it meant, wondering who I was to Luke and who he was to me and where it was going, what was coming and how soon, and was it love that was coming, maybe, maybe.

○

That weekend I went to meet my family in London, we went to an exhibition about communication. There were lots of photos of the earth layered with photos of robotic structures illustrating the expanding reach of communication, and then a room full of hundreds of radios talking at cross-purposes to one another illustrating, paradoxically, the limits of communication. My family were not happy on that day, everyone was angry and self-destructively disinterested in making the day nice. I felt that I contained a special glowing secret within me about communication and joy and how easy those things were to access. No one understood how easy it was! My favourite part of the day was the train journey back, seeing all the windows into rooms lit up, lit up so warmly and welcoming me in, really welcoming me in before they passed behind me into darkness. There were so many rooms I could enter, endless rooms lying there waiting for me.

○

On Sunday Luke messaged me asking if I could meet him in the kitchen, he wanted my opinion on some girls he was talking to on his phone. I stood in the kitchen and looked at photos of girls without really seeing them because my mind was working so hard to reconfigure itself and adjust to some new horrible reality in which Luke showed me photos of girls. That was what reality looked like now, that was what this wooden kitchen was for, for me to stand in as I saw photos of girls on Luke's cracked Android screen. Even as I stood there I was feeling a sickening pull towards him, he was wearing a tight pair of jeans and I found it really hard not to look at the crotch of those jeans as if I was a stupid and detestable animal, I really felt nauseous feeling myself standing there looking at the girls and then at Luke's jeans, looking back and forth between those two destructive visual fields endlessly. I felt on some unconscious level that those were the only things I would see for the whole rest of my life, those girls and Luke's jean crotch repeating on and on forever. I would die and my consciousness would be frozen in the form of those two images projected endlessly onto the black screens of my eyelids, that was the feeling that I had inside my stomach as I stood there in the kitchen.

Looking at the girls, I couldn't understand what united them as the objects of Luke's desire. They didn't look similar to each other at all, they fitted into completely different aesthetic worlds. Some of them were standing in bikinis drinking cocktails through straws and then some of them wore really complex unusual outfits and carried things like fake Ikea bags, I could tell that they were fake because they were very tiny like handbags. Two separate girls had these tiny fake Ikea bags. Some of the girls looked like they would be kind and some of them looked like they would be unkind. None of them looked like me, even though I didn't look specific in any way at all. I said I liked the look of all the girls and that I didn't have a favourite, which was true, I really didn't.

Back in my room I felt hot inside in a totally unfamiliar way. My body was trembling and I had the inaccurate thought that this was the first time my body did something I hadn't asked it to. I felt the alien urge to punch something and I listened to the urge and punched the blank white wall beside my door. Punching the wall did make me feel better. It made me feel better to see my despair actualised in the form of a dent in my wall, to see thin flakes of paint falling down onto the carpet and to know that the wall would need repainting because of my own personal capacity to cause harm, a capacity which was contingent upon nothing and which could not be taken from me.

○

The next morning I was woken by my own panting, I really woke up panting, gasping for breath there in my bed. As soon as I got up the panting stopped and I just felt very numb and empty but at the same time wild and almost rabid. I didn't know what to do with that feeling, I just ate a whole box of Ritz crackers until my throat was totally gummed up. I spent hours looking through Luke's Facebook friends, clicking on the Facebook profile of every girl in Luke's friend list and looking at each photo of that girl and really hating her, really hating every girl, even Luke's sisters I implausibly hated. I had never felt so stupid before, like a stupid character in a sexist romantic comedy movie. It was unbearable, I had unbearable jealous feelings and then hated myself for the jealousy, and the meaningless web of conflicting hatreds it produced.

By the evening that depressed mood was still there and eliminating my anxiety almost completely so I went and joined the literary society's pub crawl. Lots of people ignored me but some people went to great lengths to show that I was included in the group and very welcome. Millie kept saying I'm so glad you're here in a maternal way even though we didn't know each other at all. Stephen kept making jokes while looking at me even though the jokes were obviously addressed to everyone and in no way targeted at me personally, lots of them I didn't even understand because they were about things like specific members of the English faculty.

Robin was in a really energetic mood and kept doing an impression of some creature called Man-Bat, I think it was a creature from the Marvel franchise. They kept screeching in this raw high voice, Man-Bat, Man-Bat, on and on. I did find the impression funny but somehow it also depressed me. I had this really vivid sense of Man-Bat as some desperate creature, jealous of, and also lustful for, human corporeality, but endlessly trapped in this awful and repulsive veiny bat form. I kept picturing Man-Bat standing outside a bar surrounded by terrible grey smoke, looking dejected.

○

Anna and I had a seminar about vision. It turned out that if you sent electric signals to some part of a monkey's brain, the monkey's eyes would move around a lot. Me and Anna couldn't picture this, Anna said You mean the eyes just move randomly, and it was true, they really did. Somehow this was hilarious to me, the idea of the monkey's eyes moving around without any kind of target or focus. I laughed a lot even though it was a seminar, I laughed an unhinged amount and once I'd stopped I could feel that my eyes were full of tears and that some of the tears were falling down my face, streaking my cheeks. Suddenly I didn't understand what was funny at all about that monkey, suddenly the monkey's crazy eyes seemed like the saddest thing imaginable.

After the seminar I remembered a game I had created

for myself as a child. In the game I wrote out a long list of random instructions – go left, go up, go round – and then followed the instructions by myself inside my bedroom. I would end up somewhere like on top of the bedside table facing the wall, or at the bottom of the wardrobe with my face pressed to the doors. Wherever I landed, I knew that that place had been fated, that my journey had been made for me by fate. Somehow that memory gave me the same feeling as the monkey thing.

○

Luke sent me a message, the message was a gif of the Kellogg's tiger standing behind metal bars. It looked like the tiger was inside of a tennis court and it was waving sadly out, waving its paw back and forth on a depressing endless loop. Then two minutes later Luke had written Hellooo do you want to have dinner sometime??

We met in the kitchen that evening and made dinner together. I was being very quiet and almost sullen but Luke was compensating for that by being quite physical, he had found some kind of Halloween skull and was tossing it between his hands and tasting all the food we were making constantly, practically every minute he had a new bite of the food. I was playing music from my phone and then an advert for running machines came on and Luke went over to my phone and skipped the advert.

That did cheer me up, Luke feeling entitled to touch my phone screen like that, somehow that feeling of shared ownership really cheered me up a lot and I didn't feel so angry with him then.

As we were having dinner somebody knocked on Luke's door. It was two men with shaved heads and New Balance trainers. Each man had an earring in his left ear. It turned out that these were Luke's computer friends, Callum and David. God, there were so many of these stunning, lanky and very frightening men around, and they all loved computers, it was really surprising to me. Luke offered Callum and David some of the dinner we had made and they sat there on Luke's bed eating it without really looking at me. Luke didn't introduce me which somehow made me want to cry: what steps did I have to take to be deserving of a place within Luke's life, I really didn't know at all.

I felt that the right thing to do in this situation was to leave immediately and take all of the dirty plates and bowls with me to wash up alone in the brightly lit and totally unatmospheric kitchen with some morose soundtrack playing. Luke seemed surprised and actually alarmed by this idea and he kept saying No no you can stay but that sentence depressed me even more and I really did need to leave then, I was finding it hard to speak and use my face with Callum and David just sitting there on the bed.

As I was washing up I started thinking about how strange it was, that Luke had felt like this eternally tender and giving presence to me just a week earlier and had become, very suddenly, this frightening enemy in my mind, this person with a totally insatiable capacity to hurt and even destroy me. I had never felt that way about anyone else and I wondered if it was because Luke was a man. That added some very frightening dimension to things, that really shattered some potential for closeness. That was how I felt, in that moment: that being a girl opened up unbearable possibilities for being despised and denigrated, for being rejected on some painful and devastating basis, rejected for a reason I might never understand at all. The chasm between us was already there, the floor over the chasm was just waiting to collapse. That was what I thought then in a silent wordless way: I just saw the chasm.

○

I went to a lecture on embodied cognition. Embodied cognition turned out to be the way in which our bodily experience impacts our thoughts. For example, if a person is standing on a steep slope, they will see some point in the distance as further away than they would if they were standing on flat ground. This is because the body knows that uphill distances feel long, that bodily knowledge informs our perception of space. Therefore robots cannot think: that was the conclusion of the lecture.

The embodied cognition lecture was very discouraging to me. It pretended to be about human thought being enriched by embodiment but all it really said was that having a body makes our thought completely biased and stupid. Obviously the body was something very limiting, it wasn't in any way enhancing. I knew this fact already but I didn't want it to be pedagogically drilled into me, I didn't want to have to write an essay about the great tragedy of having a body.

○

That week Elon Musk invented a brain implant which allowed people to control computers with their minds. He put the implant inside a lot of pigs but most of the pigs died. Some people speculated, also, that it might be impossible to control computers with one's mind because the mind was not the same thing as the brain. I put this example into my essay on embodied cognition, I wrote: Musk's new invention relies on the assumption that we can control our brains with our minds and ignores the gulf which may exist between the physical brain and the metaphysical mind. In response to this point my supervisor wrote Evidence needed!! but it didn't seem like the kind of point which evidence could really support or refute. I didn't know what kind of evidence would address the question of whether or not an unbridgeable gulf existed between the physical brain and the metaphysical mind.

○

I didn't know how to make myself feel better that week, I didn't know what options I had, what possible acts I could engage in. I started rereading *The Catcher in the Rye*. At school that book had always cheered me up, I had identified myself with Holden somehow and found his voice really delightful and encouraging, but this time it made me feel worse, it made me feel very alone. Every sentence I read, I read in Luke's voice, even though it made no sense because Luke never said things like Goddam or Oh boy or Get your dirty stinking moron knees off my chest. I started feeling like Luke and Holden had this special private understanding which I would be left outside of forever. I could imagine them talking on and on about Jane together, on and on about how her mouth was always a little bit open and never really closed.

○

I tried to become drunk by myself, I bought a very cheap bottle of red wine and just sat on the floor drinking it without even doing anything, I really just sat there in silence completely passively and motionlessly except for the motion of bringing the bottle to and from my mouth. It took me a long time to finish it and at the end I couldn't even tell if I was drunk or not except that it felt slightly heavy to stand up from the floor, I had to reach out for the desk chair to support me. I didn't understand how people could drink by themselves, how a person could know that they were drunk when they were completely alone and therefore trapped in their own sealed mind. Surely being drunk was about the way you were with other people, about the things you said and the way you moved your body in relation to the world. It made no phenomenological sense at all in the context of being alone.

○

I went for an aimless walk over fields, I walked over lots of muddy fields by my block and eventually I found some empty swimming pool. It was painted this bright aqua blue but it was still very obvious that it was just a horrible shell of something, it was full of broken leaves and little pieces of litter, little crisp packets everywhere, Monster Munch crisp packets with lurid pictures of monsters all over them, that swimming pool really depressed me. I noticed a condom lying all bunched up inside itself as if a man had ripped it from his body in a great and frantic rush. I could really picture that man just standing there inside the pool, whipping the condom from his throbbing body swollen with aggressive sexual feeling. In that moment I wanted nothing more than to escape sex forever, sex felt like some horrible extension of those girls from the internet right then and I was very glad to be back inside my room and alone. Nothing in my room was about sex, not the carpet made of separate strands of gross brown fluff, not my folders or my raincoat, not the suicide beam which hung itself above everything.

○

For many days I stayed inside my room just looking up at the scraps of sky I could see through the windows. I ate a huge amount of food on those days, I think I ate a whole packet of Sainsbury's white chocolate and raspberry cookies on each individual day. It was hard to find any kind of reason not to sit around and eat all day. All my life my body had borne no relation to the things I put inside it, it felt like I could eat anything at any time and it would really do nothing. My actions were so free of consequences.

One day I went out to go and buy more cookies and a man swerved his bike towards me and shouted You fucking twat as he ran over my toe slightly. For a while I was almost happy that this had happened, it was almost nice to have some objectively unpleasant event in my life, to be able to nurse that slightly sore toe in my room and feel I had been wronged and even violated. But then I had some stupid nightmare that a man had run me over very badly and my whole body needed replacing like in the unsuccessful remake of RoboCop, I guess the experience had frightened me a bit.

○

Finally Luke messaged me, he said Do you want dinner I have so many leftovers we can have! I realised, when I saw his message, that I had been feeling like Luke and I would never see each other again, I had been walking through the past few days in some awful grey dream and suddenly I wasn't angry with him anymore or even with myself and I wrote back Yes!!!! and had a shower immediately with some mint-flavoured shower gel which was so cleansing that it burned my skin. I loved the sharpness of that shower gel right then, I really felt purified by that, I felt transformed even.

Luke's leftovers were various, there was sweet potato curry and then pasta with this homemade very flavoursome pesto, I said truthfully You really are the best cook I know and he laughed. He said I felt like you found it awkward when my friends came in the other night, I'm sorry about that, and I said No no you don't need to be sorry, I'm just shy. Luke laughed a lot then, and I did too, and I had meant it to be funny, shyness was such a childish concept and it was hilariously obvious that it wasn't at all the best way of describing how I'd felt. Somehow that inaccuracy really was funny to us.

Luke started telling me about some feelings he had of almost frightening alienation from himself, it seemed like this was a way of making the shyness thing okay for me, Luke telling me that he also hated being seen. He said it really freaked him out, the idea that if something happened to him, if he died for example, the newspaper would say A man has died, they would call him that, a man. It wasn't that he wasn't a man, but still the concept of being some man and having that external and objective form was very alienating to him. He said I've never even come close to trying to explain that to anyone before.

It was almost a paradox: as Luke and I were sitting on his floor talking about this I was feeling myself becoming actually very legible and very clearly defined, I really was feeling like I could be quite specifically and accurately categorised as a girl sat there beside him in my T-shirt. I was there inside my body and the way that I looked sitting there probably did very accurately reflect my internal reality of sitting and watching Luke speak inside his room as we ate all of the food that he had cooked. Some great transition was occurring inside me, something was aligning, I could actually feel it, I could feel it tangibly.

For some reason after dinner I asked Luke to cut my hair. I did want a haircut but mostly I was so enthralled by the image I could suddenly see of myself there on Luke's floor with his hands in my hair and on my shoulders and neck and with him bringing about some observable change in me. We decided on a haircut that would end at my jawline or just beneath the ends of my ears, this was almost Luke's own haircut, I had noticed this before and noticed how he would tuck his hair behind his ears but sometimes a few pieces of hair would come untucked and those pieces would come to fall around his face and would end just above the gentle fold of his top lip. I had noticed this so many times, I was so well acquainted with how this haircut fell.

I sat down on the carpet with my legs crossed and Luke sat to the side of me and held a piece of my hair there at the edge of my face. He slid two fingers around the hair so that the rest of his fingers were lightly grazing the top of my neck, the back of his hand brushing my cheekbone. I felt myself become wet and somehow that wasn't embarrassing or even notable to me, and Luke was running his scissors through the piece of hair he was holding there and so much hair was falling onto my legs and Luke's legs, too, inches of hair lying on top of us and around us, and Luke was separating out more and more sections of hair and holding them tenderly between his fingers and cutting right through them. He was behind my head then, I could feel his fingers resting there against the nape of my neck and I started with the shock of that, it really sent some kind of current right through me and I felt in that moment that Luke, too, must have felt it, that the shock must have passed straight from my body into his.

I could perceive a tangible lightening of weight then and my hair was making an almost imperceptible beating sound as it landed on the ground until suddenly Luke was finished. Immediately he said Oh shit is it way too short I'm so sorry but even this exclamation sent some hot wet shock through me and I said No I love it without even looking at it, I could tell that I loved it just by feeling it, just by running my fingers from the top of my skull to the sharp abrupt end of my hair which Luke himself had created, every ending created by Luke. He said It actually does suit you a lot and we looked in the mirror then and he was right, it really did suit me, I really loved how I looked there in Luke's bedroom mirror, stood beside him with the top of my head only just meeting his chest, both of us smiling in the mirror and with all that hair around our feet.

○

That night as I was lying in bed it was suddenly obvious that there was no danger at all, that I could be hurt but that Luke would never hurt me, that all he could do was open me and open me and that I would always be open to him, wide open and completely soft like a small trembling animal held in two hands, two hands which could crush it completely but which would not, which never would. If those hands did crush me then it would be some accident and no one would be blamed, everyone was blameless and holding each other softly and cautiously, holding each other very tenderly there on Luke's floor. It was good to give up and to soften. I really did feel a change inside my body right then. I could perceive some muscles very deep inside me letting go of some resistance, of some drive to panic.

○

The next day I woke up at six, I didn't feel tired at all and spent a long morning drinking coffee and eating oranges at my desk, writing up ideas for my dissertation. After several hours like that I went to a lecture on the history of electricity. When electricity was first discovered or invented it had been called animal magnetism. People were opposed to the idea of any electric apparatus like a telephone pole for example existing in public, they found these things very ugly. Yet still people loved to demonstrate electricity's existence through great public experiments. For example, a boy was suspended from the ceiling on silk ropes and an electric current was passed from his shoes into a girl standing beside him on top of a tar-covered barrel. The lecture slides said, about that girl: Her hand is probably extended to attract feathers or small pieces of paper. It was almost like the lecture was designed to be whimsical rather than educational or in any way clear, it didn't tell a story but still I loved that lecture, I loved seeing the old engraved illustrations of electrical currents which were always drawn as very straight lines running between things, always two things exactly, very straight lines running from one thing right into the heart of another.

○

That night Luke knocked on my door, he was crying and had just seen Mia on the bridge which led to town. He had stopped and pretended to tie his shoelaces so they hadn't acknowledged each other and when he looked up Mia was gone, he couldn't see her behind him, he couldn't see her anywhere. Somehow Luke felt that this was the last time he would ever see her, he felt that in that moment something had been killed and lost forever. I said Luke you'll see her again, you will see her again for sure, I said Nothing is final, nothing is ever destroyed, I didn't know where I was pulling these ideas from or if I really meant anything I was saying but in that moment it did feel true:

nothing could die, everything would live on forever in some possible future and each future was real.

Luke and I watched, then, the programme where lots of gay men gave people and houses makeovers. It felt quite important, what we were watching, and quite beautiful, the idea of all those people and houses being improved, made clearer, made more real. We watched new sofas being purchased, some new clocks and some new blankets. Everything could be bought, everything could be made new and the houses looked much nicer then, so much larger and much lighter even though nothing structural had changed at all.

That whole evening Luke was wearing a small pair of pyjama shorts and as we were sitting there I was subtly and almost unconsciously trying to memorise the position of each freckle on his legs, I was trying to memorise every constellation of freckles until for some reason I felt this great shot of loss, this sudden thirsty and bereft feeling as if I was seeing something I was already mourning and I leaned my face behind his shoulder slightly so I couldn't see his legs anymore. As I did that Luke shifted his weight almost imperceptibly into mine and I knew very suddenly that I had been right, that nothing could be lost and that everything was real. It really was true to me, lying there with Luke's legs invisible to me but with our bodies softly pushing at each other's seams.

○

I had a dream that I was sitting on the top floor of the library. I looked down towards the entrance and saw Mia walk in and I knew, in the dream, that the second she entered the library I had to jump off the balcony. Somehow if I didn't do that I would never see Mia again and in the dream that was the worst thought imaginable, that thought really made me want to kill myself so there was no question, of course I would jump. I guess I had been Luke in the dream. Then I had a second dream that Mia and I were sitting in an empty bathtub together and Mia said something cryptic about me being a baby. In the dream the baby comment was really flattering and then we looked up from the bathtub into a window through the brick wall ahead of us and there was a lava lamp sitting in the windowsill, so much golden wax drifting slowly around in great soft bulbs inside the lava lamp's glass cage. That was beautiful to see, that was breathtakingly beautiful.

I felt so lucky when I woke up, I had experienced so much. It was already light, the sun was really streaming in then.

○

I went to a lecture about structuralism. It turned out that structuralism meant symbolism. There was some idea that everything stood for some other thing. Things were connected within systems and the relationships between the things within the systems stood for other, more real, relationships, within other systems. An example is that certain animals are seen as fit for eating and others are not. Really fit for eating means holy and not fit for eating means abominable. Abominable things often live in the water, or they might creep or swarm. For example we would never eat a snake or wasp. Those things are not fit for the table, let alone the altar. That was how the lecture went.

I found the whole lecture totally compelling, my heart was really beating hard as I sat there listening to it. The things I heard aligned with some deep-rooted feeling I had that everything was so much heavier than it appeared to be, everything carried within it some great weight, some concealed and central core meaning. There were ideas like abominableness and holiness hidden within everything, even things that seemed like nothing. In the end everything would be weighed down with meaning. People would look back and see that they had missed the point completely, that they had really understood nothing.

○

That week Anna got tonsillitis, she called me and together we called 111 and unexpectedly they told us to go straight to A&E. This was quite thrilling to both of us, Anna's tonsils hurt for sure but she was basically fine and it felt like something out of a film, to us, to be sitting in a taxi on the way to A&E in the middle of some normal afternoon, that felt very intense and very gripping.

We waited in A&E for a long time until it was dark outside and the hospital building we could see out through the window was lit up against the sky, I could see a row of plants standing in the bright windows of that hospital building. We ate lots of chocolates from the vending machines and then eventually an old man called us into a consultation room. The old man said How are you feeling in yourselves, he addressed this question to both of us and it was funny but also moving to me, this weirdly emotional question the old man doctor asked us. After I said I felt fine and Anna said she had tonsillitis the doctor prescribed her antibiotics and we went back to our rooms.

○

I bumped into Adam and Robin in the university canteen the next night and ended up going back to Adam's room with them. I couldn't tell if I had been invited or if I was forcing myself into that encounter but I almost didn't care, somehow I did very badly want to sit with them in Adam's room, because I felt happy, so I didn't have to be alone and suffer. They were having a conversation about gender and Robin was saying that no one at the literary society introduces themselves with their pronouns except for Robin themself, none of the cis people bothered saying their pronouns at all. This was a good point and I felt bad that I hadn't considered it before, I made a mental note to say my pronouns in the next meeting.

It wasn't entirely straightforward to me, though, this question of gender. Before Luke I had never really felt gendered, I had never felt I was producing some gendered version of myself through living. A loose gendered sheen had been added to my life, things had some rich new meaning which was gender, it was my gender in interaction with Luke's. There was this charged glow between us which was dependent upon me being a girl and him not being one, and which in turn made me even more of a girl somehow, and him even less of one. It sounded very heterosexual when I thought of it like that but it didn't feel depressingly heterosexual at all. It felt incredibly new, like something Luke and I were inventing ourselves. Every look was new, every touch, even touching a chair was new, I thought as I sat in Adam's chair.

I didn't know how to communicate that feeling with Adam and Robin and I felt that it was probably not relevant, it was obviously much more trivial than real issues of gender and discrimination. But at the same time I did feel that a tangible change in my gender was taking place, some real change which was in fact deeply relevant to

Butler's ideas of performance, to gender itself as any meaningful category. I was performing something new, now. I really didn't know what I was going to become.

○

Luke knocked on my door the next morning to ask my opinion on a T-shirt he had bought, he had been for a walk around the city and had walked into a shop. It was a secondhand T-shirt, dark grey and quite nondescript, I wasn't sure how he could be uncertain about it and I kept saying It looks great, it looks great until eventually I said Luke shut up it's just some T-shirt and he laughed a lot then and seemed more certain of the T-shirt.

For a while we stood beside each other in front of my long mirror just looking at ourselves and at each other, looking at Luke in his new generic T-shirt. This was the second memory I had of me and Luke stood side by side within a pane of glass. Now both of our mirrors had seen us stood together. Luke said Whenever I look in the mirror I do this face, he showed me the face and it was true, he was doing a slight pout and tilting his face a bit upwards, he wasn't quite looking straight at himself. He said it was alarming, the fact that he would never know what his real face looked like, he would only ever see his mirror face. I said What about photos but somehow we decided that photos weren't the same, in some way photos too were very fake to us right then. I said Your real face looks so good and that was hilarious to us as we stood there right in front of the mirror. That was some great gift, to have that speech act met with laughter.

○

Suddenly then it was the holidays. Luke and I had breakfast together before our families came to take us home, we went to a cafe opposite the history of art department and ordered elaborate pancakes which came littered with small flowers, small violets. Luke said Hey would you want to do phone calls over Christmas and then he bought me an expensive cappuccino and I said nothing during this whole exchange, I just grinned with delight and accepted these things, the phone calls, the coffee, I was laughing with delight as I accepted these things into my life.

On the way back to our rooms we bumped into Luke's mother, she was carrying a box of pears. It seemed like the pears had come straight from Luke's garden although maybe they were just some pears from a shop. I took a pear and ate it right there in the parking lot, I said to Luke's mother Oh it's delicious with some juice dripping slightly down my chin and Luke laughed loudly and said Really. Luke's mother handed me another pear then.

I wasn't at all upset on the car ride home. Somehow it felt like the start of some new chapter and that was very thrilling to me, the idea of some new chapter, some new chapter in which Luke and I would talk and talk through the phone until we were reunited inside a shared physical context in the spring. Somehow that felt fine and not at all distressing to me, in that moment physical location seemed so trivial and almost fake as I sat there in the car and watched so many sunlit fields pass the windows, roadsides, ugly service stations which were nothing to do with me and which disappeared in practically a minute, there was nothing I had to see out of the windows for any extended period of time.

It was difficult to talk about my term on that car ride, it was difficult to communicate anything. I said And I made a new friend Luke but this sentence really communicated nothing of the richness of the thing, everything was incommunicable and some warm throbbing secret and that wasn't painful to me either as I sat watching the scenery all disappear behind me.

○

That whole holiday was like a dream, a golden dream set in some dappled field. I had never seen a winter which was so yellow before, the cold made everything so crisp and somehow gleaming, all the leafless branches glowing. Luke and I had so many phone conversations while walking through parks or along rivers round our separate homes, separately clutching our phones to our ears. My phone was always greasy from my face and streaked with the imprints of strands of my hair and it was wonderful, it was so lovely to take out my phone when I got home and see that physical evidence of our intimacy, I really loved that dirt all over my phone. I loved, too, that Luke and I were apart and therefore able to describe our surroundings to each other in endless detail, I loved having my mental images filtered through his consciousness: I wasn't seeing a dog or a man but Luke's impressions of that dog or man. It was amazing to me, that mediation, it made me so full of love for everything, each little dog scratching Luke's shoes. I felt that I was really seeing the world, when Luke described it to me through the phone.

Because it was the holidays our lives were paused and we were almost children again, doing nothing except looking at our hometowns, eating meals with our families. And so Luke wanted to speak a lot about childhood, or other disconnected things from the past. This, too, was so pleasing to me and made me feel even more like we were together inside of some shared dream or shared canopied bed outside of time. There was nothing I wanted to listen to more than Luke's childhood neuroses.

He told me about his childhood insecurity about freckles. He was so insecure about his freckles that one year he stayed inside all summer to stop new freckles from forming. It was so depressing when a new freckle appeared, he said, so depressing seeing the freckle and knowing it would be with you for months or even years, sitting stupidly on your face and totally unkillable.

He told me, too, a story about basketball. Luke had broken his finger playing basketball at school and when he broke his finger he thought Now this is another thing that's wrong with me. When he told his mother this she had said No, you are gorgeous. This story filled me with a vague but really pressing sense of longing and eventually I understood that it was because I, too, wanted to be able to say to Luke No, you are gorgeous when he told me all the things he found so wrong about himself. Before this basketball anecdote I had found the word gorgeous somehow stupid or even a bit revolting but suddenly it was clear to me that it was vital, it really communicated something very specific and fundamental, it communicated something I desperately did want to communicate.

○

My family had an announcement to share, we were moving house, we were moving to a slightly smaller house on the other side of the city. Everyone seemed really anxious when they told me this, I was surprised at first by how anxious everyone seemed but then I remembered that at some point in the past this announcement would have upset me quite a lot. I had been very fussy about my things at some point in the past. But now I really didn't care, I didn't mind where my things went or what happened to them. I started putting things in boxes, my old toys, old books and teenage clothes, random ornaments and folded paper things. After I put these things into a box I couldn't remember if the box had been for things I wanted to take with me or things I wanted to throw out. The distinction seemed almost arbitrary somehow: precious things from my life's past, and useless trash.

○

I became very interested in studying in cafes, practically every day I would go to some cafe and sit there doing readings for the next term's lectures. I would sit inside the cafe eating and eating and then I would go speak to Luke, I would call him from the park in the centre of town and walk from there along the river. I would keep walking for miles along that river, or I'd turn and loop the park again, if it was empty there, if it was raining on that day for example or extremely cold. Sometimes I'd curl up beneath a tree so I saw nothing except tree trunk and fallen leaves and my own trousers, I would sit there hugging my knees and talk and talk to Luke through the phone.

One evening I got home after a day of talking to Luke and walking up and down all the rivers round the city and I saw that my feet were completely destroyed by these huge blisters, blisters so bloody they glued my feet into their socks. It was amazing, how talking to Luke made me forget pain completely. It was the opposite of self-harm, the pain an imperceptible and actually irrelevant side effect. There was pain but I didn't care at all, there were so many things so much more important than pain.

○

Then it was Christmas Day. I couldn't believe that Christmas still existed, Christmas felt like something out of the past somehow or out of some childish movie. I had forgotten to get anyone anything, even cards I had completely forgotten about, I felt really bad about that and didn't know how to make it better or explain it even, I tried to make it better by just ignoring it. I drank lots of Prosecco, I played so many rounds of charades with surprising confidence and almost with delight, I really did enjoy using my hands and face to make all those explanatory gestures at my grandmother's table. All my relatives seemed surprised by me, happily surprised, I couldn't tell if it was because I wasn't wearing jeans and some horrible sweatshirt or because I wasn't being shy, I was being extremely loud, I was shouting and gesticulating wildly and no one seemed angry that I didn't have a gift for them.

○

Something happened to my ears that holiday, they became totally clogged up with an impenetrable layer of earwax and I could hear just vaguely from my left ear and not at all from my right one. I felt this great pressure in my head as if something very thick and heavy was building up and in urgent need of outlet, it felt laborious to even turn or tilt my head. The morning it started I lay in bed crying in an awful breathy way at the thought that Luke and I would be unable to communicate, he would speak and I wouldn't hear him and would have to keep asking What? What? until the conversation was impossible and one or both of us gave up. I really felt that that might happen as I lay there in my single bed: that something between me and Luke might die right there because of this problem with my ears.

But when Luke called me it seemed that I could hear him completely when I held the phone to my left ear. Somehow the specificity of the sound coming through my phone's tiny speaker made his voice more audible than the sounds in my immediate environment, so his voice was all I heard, Luke's voice inside some new intimate soundscape. Sometimes he heard sounds coming from my side of the phone that I hadn't heard myself, some birdsong, some siren, he would tell me and I would say Oh really and look around for the bird or the police car or ambulance, and often those things would be completely out of sight and impossible to find, they had already gone off somewhere in some other direction and were making their way to someplace very far away from me.

After a few days my ears fixed themselves, orange liquid trickled out in the night and seeped into my pillow and spread itself a bit over my cheeks. I washed it off in the shower and the problem was fixed then, it was finished.

○

Luke was seeing his childhood friend Max a lot that week. Max was hilarious, Luke said, and great at tennis; he had so many pet rats, Luke thought that we would really get on. He said he had told Max lots about me, he had said to Max Me and her get on like a house on fire. When Luke told me this my heart did a kind of double beat, I stood there in the centre of the park really grinning to myself for a long time surrounded by the deserted sunlit grass. Luke was so right, that was exactly how well we got on, like some very bright transmuting force, a great structure of walls burning right down to the ground.

The holiday was over then, and the next time I came home it would be to a different house: this was a fascinating thought. Never again would I see my childhood bedroom with its view of the old dilapidated garden shed, never again would I see that row of horse chestnut trees behind the garden, those sticky and revolting trees dropping their spiked nuts everywhere. Maybe ten years ago I had been really obsessed with climbing onto the roof of my shed and from that roof into the trees, I had some fantasy of standing right at the top of one of those trees entirely hidden in its leaves but it was obviously impossible, the branches on those trees were very sparse, there would be a whole metre or two without any branches at all and it was impossible to scale those branchless sections.

I remembered then a time when I was maybe nine or ten and had buried a pair of my knickers in the garden of the house behind the trees. Somehow that had felt very thrilling to me, leaving my knickers in that stranger's garden, and maybe the knickers had been dirty, slightly soiled, I think that was some part of it. I had wanted to put a contaminated part of myself into a place which was not mine, I could understand that still, I could really understand that.

I sent Luke a photo of the view from my window, the shed and row of trees and my waterlogged and bad-looking childhood garden. He sent back a photo of a Lego tower he had standing in his bedroom, it was really tall and made of very plain bricks except for a Lego ambulance randomly positioned in its centre. I could tell that Luke was older than me from the plainness of his Lego bricks, none of my Lego had ever been that plain. If I made a tower from my childhood Lego it would need a balcony on every floor to use up all the abortive bricks, the bricks onto which nothing could slot down at all, bricks ending in steering wheels or little orange flames of fire. All the golden plastic tridents from the lost and sunken city of Atlantis.

○

Luke and I arrived back the next day, he knocked on my door before he had even unpacked anything and when I opened the door he was standing there surrounded by so many boxes, so many piles of coats and jumpers, so many plants, that was some heavenly scene and I flung myself straight into him. It was wonderful, to hug someone so tall, to hug someone and have my face disappear into their chest, to breathe and know that in breathing I was breathing in that person, their T-shirt, their scent, there was nothing I would rather breathe into myself. When the hug ended I did some strange punch to Luke's shoulder to push him away, it really felt in that moment like if the hug was going to end I had to force it to end quite violently and Luke laughed at that but he didn't look confused at all. That felt very loving to me in that moment, that gentle acceptance from Luke as I pushed him away through his shoulder.

We went for a walk then through the freezing sunlit day. It was strange, I had almost forgotten what it felt like to be walking with Luke as a physical presence there beside me, I associated walking now with his disembodied phone voice. I was distracted by the constant question of our proximity to each other, I was constantly monitoring whether we were getting further away from one another as we walked there by the river, whether we were getting further or possibly closer until finally Luke took my arm in his. As he did this he made some comment about it being cold as if he was taking my arm for the sake of our survival in the outside air – carefully he was ensuring that his actions were linked with the material world and I admired this, I could see that that linguistic sophistication made almost anything possible and maybe that was something I could learn, that subtlety, that potency, maybe those things could grow inside of me and make some new future possible.

I could feel something inside me pulse and tremble as I walked with Luke's arm linked through mine, I could feel that tangibly and I let myself be carried by it as Luke and I walked there by the river and talked, I think, about skin problems. I really think we were talking about skin problems as we walked beside the river, I think Luke was telling me about how he blamed every hard thing in his life on having bad skin. Somehow he felt that reality might be organised differently if he had better skin, I really think that was what we were talking about in that moment, about the possible but improbable importance of skin.

○

I saw Mia again that week, I saw her in the supermarket vegetarian substitute foods aisle. She was wearing a beautiful long coat and had these square sunglasses resting on her head and sort of holding her hair back very delicately, I said Hi in a low voice like I was about to cough and Mia said Oh hi and gave me an actually very warm smile, I felt almost welcomed into something by that smile and immediately left the vegetarian substitute foods aisle and checked out my stupid basket of easy peelers and bread and Crunchy Nut at the self-service checkouts without looking at any other person, really without looking back towards Mia at all.

I felt very bad about myself that afternoon, I felt very guilty about the way that I was feeling towards Mia. Because really I was feeling some kind of almost irresistible pull towards her, really I did very badly want to talk to her and to tell her the things that I was feeling. I wanted Mia to tell me the future, I wanted her to tell me if he was going to love me and how soon and what would that look like, how would I know. I wanted her to tell me what his body looked like, I wanted her to tell me all the things he said when he was angry and wanted to cause harm, the things he said when he was hurt, the things he said to someone who could really hurt him. I almost felt that these were questions I could actually ask Mia, because we were both girls. But obviously lots of things were much deeper than gender. Me and Mia were not on the same side of anything.

○

Me and Luke had dinner that night and talked about sex. Luke said that in sex he was some fake person, he really acted differently, he said things he would never say in a normal conversation, he was actually unrecognisable. This idea upset me so much that I became almost choked up, I kept asking in a choked and high-pitched voice But is that what you want or just what you think the other person wants. Somehow I felt that of course Luke wanted to have a kind of sex which aligned with who he was when we talked to each other, somehow I was certain that I knew his fundamental self and that he could have no other real or plausible ways of being. Luke said that he just couldn't see any other way of doing it, he said that occasionally in sex some reality would break through and it would ruin it, suddenly the things he was saying and doing would feel crude and actually ridiculous, they would feel almost horrible. One time he said to Mia Touch your pussy and for a second then he felt really revolting for having said that, he had to stay in the sex mode of being or he would start to feel bad at things like that and sex would be impossible, it would be terrible, it just wouldn't make sense.

This conversation really depressed me, it made me feel actually insane. I didn't understand why you couldn't just have sex without having to say Touch your pussy. In my mind sex was a rich and bursting extension of reality, sex was Luke saying I'm so sorry I have been so afraid I love you I love you and then exploding into me in a brightly lit and entirely empty room, the scale constantly expanding and collapsing so that I could see his whole body and then each tiny piece of his body as close up as I could possibly get to it, Luke's body magnified and expanded simultaneously, every freckle, each soft hair right there in front of me. And when he looked at me there would be no pain. The language of his face would be entirely legible.

○

That night I had a dream that Luke told me about a sex trick. In the trick he lifted the other person up over his head and flung them into a spectacular mid-air backflip. The person would fall, then, and land softly on the bed – and that was sex. In the dream I was so upset that Luke had shown me this sex trick, I felt that some great potential had been ruined by his demonstration and I decided to do the trick on Luke to show him that his trick wasn't so special. I picked him up and threw him but I did the thing wrong, he fell on his back in a hard sudden shock and he wouldn't wake up. I woke up panting like some nasty dog, I rolled over into the wall and stayed there for a long time trying to remove from my mind that image of Luke being thrown so violently and harshly onto his bed.

That day I was supposed to be writing an essay about the history of global warming for my history of science paper. It turned out that a French minister had discovered global warming in the 1820s. He had argued that the Earth's atmosphere traps radiant heat and that deforestation added to that heat. The heat was building up, he said, and one day, maybe soon, it would be impossible to survive in such conditions. I read a thirty-page paper about this French minister and when I was finished I realised that I was actually feeling nauseous with anxiety. I went to the bathroom then and lay down in the empty bath for a long time, trying to think about the French minister and draw some conclusions from him. Nothing seemed to relate to anything else, nothing carried any discursive weight at all and eventually I went back to my room and lay on my bed with the blinds closed and thought about nothing.

When I finally went out to make some toast in the kitchen I bumped into Luke in the corridor, he was really explicitly delighted to see me and started talking as if he was resuming some conversation we were already in the middle of and suddenly it was obvious that nothing at all was wrong, or that the things which were wrong could be easily ignored for some indefinite amount of time. I put sex to one side then, I really let myself forget about sex and I went back to my room and wrote the global warming essay easily and painlessly. When I handed it in the supervisor wrote Insightful! on the top of the first page. That Insightful! comment wasn't about any specific part of my essay, she had found the whole essay insightful, the argument, each specific piece and the way in which those pieces formed a whole. I had constructed something total and complete, and someone had looked at the thing and decided it was worthy of their praise.

Luke had to go home for some appointment on Friday and somehow I constructed a compelling argument to go with him and for us to spend the day together in his hometown. I couldn't believe that he had been persuaded, I really couldn't believe that, I felt like I had cheated my way in to some sacred experience which wasn't meant for me at all. I would see the place that Luke was from, I would see the physical bases of his most intimate, foundational memories, I really couldn't believe it and designed some outfit for the day that I thought he would like, some all-black outfit full of complex shapes. I did a sharp and cleansing facemask, I really did everything I could that Thursday night, I washed my hair a lot of separate times using separate shampoos which were just lying in the shower because I really didn't know which shampoo was the best one, that was something I had no idea about.

Luke and I took the train together early on Friday morning and listened to music from his phone through a single pair of earphones, one earphone inside each of our ears, our heads connected through the flimsy metal wires. Outside the windows were endless flooded fields, endless bridges and little canal boats all so far below the train with Luke and I just floating there above them. Occasionally I would be looking out the window at the fields and would remember with a flip of my heart that Luke was beside me and the fields would become something else entirely, something really filled up and saturated with potential and I would relax back in my seat and my shoulder would relax into Luke's side and I would smile quietly, a private smile meant either for just me and Luke or for me only, I wasn't sure.

○

Once we arrived Luke went to his appointment and I wandered randomly through streets, streets which I found difficult to link with Luke in any meaningful way, streets filled with old church buildings and little cobbled stones and then streets filled with Boots and Oxfam and The Ivy. Still it was wonderful to be in these streets which Luke must have walked through a hundred times, a hundred times even as a small child, it was staggering to think about how many times Luke must have seen that sign for The Ivy, maybe some times when he was happy, maybe some times when he was feeling terrible and entirely alone, maybe he had even sat inside of The Ivy with his family for some occasion, his sister's birthday, maybe, his parents' anniversary, I really didn't know.

Luke texted me after only about forty minutes saying that he was done, he was ready. The appointment had been uneventful, he had thought that some procedure would be necessary but it turned out not to be, he was fine and nothing had been done to him. He came to find me and we walked through streets, suddenly hysterical, hysterical about something really incommunicable, some dumb joke Luke had made about old churches, I think, some untrue facts he started spouting about churches. We were walking down the street doubled over with laughter and a small child was in front of us suddenly and trying, for some reason, to walk between us, and this child's face killed us as well, its blank and weirdly insolent expression, that killed us and we moved apart on the pavement to let the child through, moving apart while almost falling into the road with hilarity and I remember thinking I hope this child remembers us and remembers how absolutely happy we were, how entirely and straightforwardly happy. I really wanted that child to remember that somehow.

Luke took me to his favourite cafe, then, a cafe which cooked everything in beef fat, even vegetarian things, and I had no qualms at all about this beef fat cafe, I was delighted to eat some vegetarian burger and chips cooked in beef fat and that frightened me, actually, that really frightened me, that reminded me in an objective undeniable way that something qualitatively new and strange was happening but I did already know that, that wasn't something that should surprise me anymore and I ate the beef fat chips very happily and dipped them thickly into ketchup to mask the beef flavour as Luke and I sat on a tiny patch of grass laughing extremely loudly at Luke's inexplicable but visceral negative reaction towards ketchup and all wet condiments, they really revolted him and I could see it in his body, I could see him recoil and that was hilarious to us too, that visible recoiling of Luke away from my wet ketchup.

We walked, then, to a mound outside the city. Luke took two cans of warm flat beer out from his backpack and we sat and drank them on the hillside with the whole city spread out beneath us, and in that moment I really adored warm and flat beer, I really preferred it, it felt like the beer had come straight from my body and that in drinking it I was simply returning it to its original and foundational place inside of me.

As we sat there Luke pointed out the landmarks of his past, his parents' house, his old school, his sister's old school, the pitches on which he had played football as a teenager. I saw them all so far beneath me, shrunken, and it was impossible to imagine that these places were real, that they were anything more than a scene Luke had created in order to give it to me right then on this specific day as we sat beside each other with our legs outstretched on the ground there in front of us. It really seemed that I would see those things forever, my legs and Luke's legs outstretched there and Luke's past stretched out ahead of us too. That was some eternal image, that was something very timeless. It was fine for a cow to die for that, for endless cows to die for that, it really made sense that I just couldn't care at all about those beef fat chips.

That evening we went to Luke's house, we were only going to be there for a few minutes, our train was soon. Luke's house was unexpectedly huge, it had a great extended front garden and stone steps leading up to the doorway. It felt like just inside that front garden there were endless private places to go to, endless places to walk even as I stood there in the darkness. Barely anything was visible except the light flooding out of Luke's windows and illuminating lots of stones and the barrier which lay around the steps up to the doorway.

No one in Luke's family was home and we went straight to his bedroom. Luke sat down on the bed and started tossing a small ball between his palms. I think the ball was filled with beans, it kept collapsing to fit the shape of his palms, collapsing loudly with a great rattling noise each time it hit one of his wide-open palms. There was something strange on his bookshelf, I thought it was a tiny squat teddy but he said it was actually an Egyptian organ pot he had made in school, a tiny clay pot for organs.

For some reason Luke and I exchanged a hair tie then, I took the hair tie from my hair where it was securing a tiny half-ponytail and handed it to him, and he tied his hair into a partial topknot with it. That looked very handsome, that partial topknot, I stood on Luke's floor and watched him lie back on his bed with his hair tied up like that. I felt some sudden spasm within me as I watched Luke lying there across the bed, some soft internal thing relaxing. Suddenly then it was time to go, right at that moment of unclenching. It was almost as if Luke could sense it, as if he could sense the feeling I was having right at that moment of so many different possible futures spooling out ahead of us inside his childhood bedroom, so many different futures which could have begun for us right then, right at that moment. I felt actually mournful getting on the train, I felt actually mournful even though Luke and I were getting on the train together and going to the same exact place.

○

That night my grandfather died, he had been sick for a long time and had been living in a care home for years. I felt that I had never even known him, I felt that I was too young to have really known him but I was very upset for my mother and especially afraid for my grandmother, she had always said that she would kill herself when he died even though I felt that that was the kind of twisted thing old people never said. It had almost thrilled me the first time I heard her say that, it was so shocking. I didn't know if she meant it, I really didn't know what was going to happen. I asked my mother if she wanted me to come home but she said it was fine, she said to keep going with term. She said my grandfather had wanted to donate his body to medical students but now my grandmother didn't want that, and I could understand that, actually, I could understand why the idea of some destruction of the body, some breakdown of the body into its constituent parts for medical students to analyse and cut open into even smaller parts was very distressing, almost unbearably distressing. It was important to keep one's own pieces, one's own eyes and bones. It was important to keep the pieces of the people that we loved, I didn't think my grandmother was wrong about that at all.

○

The next day I went to London by myself, I went to see a Louise Bourgeois sculpture exhibition. There were sculptures made of creepy pink cotton and then some sculptures made of smooth shining metal. The metal ones were my favourites, they felt very untouchable to me and very alien, they really seemed in that moment to be full of a great solitary longing. There was a headless metal body suspended from the ceiling, its hands stretched backwards to its ankles as it dangled there so passively like something dead. Then there was a pile of metal hands clutching at each other, almost clawing at each other, that one was called The Welcoming Hands and I felt that was sarcastic, those hands were not welcoming at all, they were desperate, they were desperately trying to hold on to one another and to hold each other back, even, they were hands in pain and they were not kind.

On the train back to university I started googling Louise Bourgeois, I spent a lot of the train journey clicking on different Wikipedia links and found an artwork she'd made on a piece of squared paper like the paper in some children's maths book, where she'd written

> I LOVE YOU
> DO YOU
> LOVE me
> ?
> YES no

It was part of a bigger series of works called *We Love You* and there were different versions of it, some of them in heavy serif lettering, some of them in watercolour cursive handwriting, endless versions of that question repeated over so many pieces of squared paper. Then I found a separate quotation from Louise Bourgeois, it said If you don't love me I am ready to attack. I am a double-edged knife. The person who was sharing that quotation had superimposed it over a photo of a sunlit ocean as if they thought it was somehow inspirational although after a while I understood that probably it was a robot that had done that, a person would never do that. It was so obvious what that quotation meant, it meant death, it really meant somebody's death, I knew as I stared into the photo of the ocean's sunlit rocks.

○

I cried a lot that night once I was back in my room and even as I was walking from the station, tears were streaming out of me in a frightening unending way, wet tears streaking my entire face and neck. At first I felt guilty that I was crying so much because of the I LOVE YOU DO YOU LOVE me? YES no, because of Luke and not because of my grandfather, but the more I cried the more obvious it seemed that everything was really the same thing, there was really only one thing and that thing was loss, the unbearable loss of things which had been very alive, things which had been full of potential and of meaning and which were gone or which were going, which were fading, moving endlessly far from me and descending into the distance like those pieces of Luke's past lying at the bottom of that hill and looking so unconvincing, looking so completely false.

The next morning I had a dissertation social in the botanic gardens, my whole dissertation group was going to meet there. As soon as I arrived I was transported into some completely new mode of behaviour and feeling, the thing about the double-edged knife and the awful loss of everything around me felt very random and like something from some kind of melodramatic stage play, it was so easy to let those things go and to stand around beneath umbrellas in the rain drinking hot chocolate with my dissertation group. For some reason I kept making jokes about Timothée Chalamet, I kept making jokes about how attractive I thought Timothée Chalamet was and everyone loved that somehow, some woman kept talking about how her partner is less attractive now he had a beard and that really elevated me, talking about Timothée Chalamet and that woman's partner's beard, those things felt very false and hilarious in that moment and nothing felt further from I LOVE YOU DO YOU LOVE me? YES no. When the social was over I practically followed everyone back to their offices, I kept walking with one group of people going to the psychology laboratory and when they arrived I ran after another pair of people who had been going to their offices in some other building and walked with them, too, until they also arrived at the place where they were going and I was alone.

The next night I had dinner with Luke, I hadn't thought that I would talk to him about how terrible I had been feeling but as soon as I saw him in the kitchen with some lovely Ottolenghi courgette fritters on the stove I knew that I would tell him, I almost felt that he already knew, he was being so sweet with me, he was saying I love your outfit even though I was just wearing random trousers and a badly-fitting T-shirt. I said Luke I'm so happy to see you, my grandad died and immediately then I was talking about the Louise Bourgeois things, The Welcoming Hands and how desperate they were, I was saying It's so dumb but I just felt that everything was going to go away from me somehow, everything was going to die or get lost. Luke's eyes were watering then, he was looking at me with a very clear straight look as his eyes really did begin to water in the kitchen. Never again would I meet a man who cried so easily, who was so easily moved to tears right in front of my eyes, really never again in my whole life. Luke said Hang on and tossed the fritters on a plate and within seconds we were inside of his room in the sink light with that great beam up above our heads.

Luke said I'm so sorry and then he said I think I understand what you're saying about that feeling of everything being about to leave you. He said When I was like eight or nine I think I was a bit depressed because of that, I just couldn't understand how people kept going when they knew that obviously everything was going to end like that, I found it really difficult to come to terms with and like with Mia, I don't know, I've been feeling it more again recently, it just seems so obvious that there's no way to hold onto anything and by the end maybe you don't even want to, you know, you don't even want those things, that's almost worse to me.

He laughed bitterly then like some cynical person in a very old movie and said I'm sorry, I've just made this about Mia when your grandad just died. I said Don't be sorry, I wasn't even thinking about my grandad – what you say is exactly it, I just feel like I don't know how to just keep something safe and feel that I really have it, you know, that it's mine and can't just slip away from me like that. Luke said Are you thinking about something in particular or is it just like a feeling and I said I don't know. There was some great pause then with Luke looking me right in the eyes, Luke seeing my eyes fill up with barely visible tears, Luke really looking at me as if he was trying to make a decision or stare very deep into the heart of something. Eventually he said Can I show you a song and I said Please with both of us still looking very far into each other's open eyes.

Luke put on the song, then, from his phone, a song by this band called The Microphones, the album cover was a cartoon elephant standing in a deep blue forest over some brightly glowing fire. The song started very quietly with this guitar plucking, you could hear somebody's fingers really sliding along the guitar strings and then a man was shouting, really shouting about this trip that he had taken to the house of the parents of someone he had loved, the trip he'd taken with that person, together they had woken up in bed in the house of those parents, they had walked to a mountain, they had lain on the sand and heard the crashing of the ocean. The man had finally felt free but it was clear in the song that these things had happened some unreachably long time ago and that he was desperately trying, now, to save himself and become new again but he couldn't, he really couldn't, he was stuck and all he had now was this terrible loss, this endless absence.

By the end of the song I really was crying, I had been listening to this man shouting about this great pain and this eternal loss for more than five minutes, with Luke sitting beside me on the floor, knees tucked to his chest, and I said Luke this is exactly what I am so scared of. Luke said Yes, me too, this song is very scary to me, then he said He really sounds so broken, it just makes me think there could be someone who could touch even more of me than Mia did. That person could really destroy me, he said.

We sat on the floor for a long time then, thinking about that lethal person who could touch all those untouchable parts of Luke. Both of us were sitting with our knees folded up to our chests and our hearts were beating electrically, beating in sync to the frightening beat of the song. Luke and I sat there breathing in and breathing out into the air which was stuck inside his room, both of us recycling that air over and over again inside his room as we sat there feeling very alive and split open by the fear. After maybe fifteen minutes of us sitting there like that I typed I love you do you love me Louise Bourgeois into Luke's phone and showed him the

I LOVE YOU
DO YOU
LOVE me
?
YES no

Luke said nothing but he screenshotted the picture, it was there, then, dormant in his Screenshots folder, sitting waiting in his Screenshots folder just like I love you do you love me was now inside of his search history, it had been put there by me. Luke said Okay let's be happy now and immediately then we were laughing at some complex impression he was doing, some kind of joke where he stuck his fist inside his T-shirt and let his whole body be dragged by the fist, his fist dragging him round the room like some great desperate heart. It was a strange joke, I wondered why Luke had thought of it.

I went to a nature reserve, it took more than an hour to walk there and somehow there was no way of reaching it by any other mode of transport but I was desperate to be in a forest, I didn't want to be in parks anymore, I wanted some tall wooden darkness. When I arrived there were too many bluebells in that forest, I had wanted endless trees and some cold orange glow which was obviously an autumn thing, obviously what I wanted was a forest in the autumn and maybe not even in England, maybe in Canada or Finland or some other place. I had to just stare upwards at the trees ascending into the whiteness of the sky. That was nice, all those bare branches fighting for light up there, fighting for space and almost eclipsing the sky with their harsh branches. I didn't see any animals, not one, and I wondered if that meant the nature reserve was failing, if it was failing to preserve nature.

That afternoon I went to a lecture on the history of our understanding of atoms and the particle model. I didn't know what the particle model was so my engagement with the lecture was mostly aesthetic. Mostly I just aesthetically admired the idea that the world was made up of substances which could not be simplified at all, items which were already in their smallest and most broken form. There really were things that could not be acted upon. I could see that this must have been a very thrilling discovery for some man to make, in the eighteenth century.

○

I thought that perhaps I had some kind of moral responsibility to test my assumption that no one could understand how I felt about Luke, I thought that I should probe at that assumption a bit in case I was wrong somehow and depriving myself of some great chance to be saved. Héloise and I went to Caffè Nero after our statistics class and I tried to explain it to her, I said He has this ex-girlfriend he still really loves but at the same time I can tell he feels there's something really big between us, I can feel some kind of energy that he's obviously also contributing to, like it's him who initiates a lot of things, whenever we touch, if we hug or something it's always him who's initiated that. I could tell that I was sounding very stupid and I was actually making myself feel so much worse reducing me and Luke's friendship like that and really misrepresenting it, really misrepresenting both of us and making it sound like some very inane situation that might be in a kind of early 2000s romantic comedy which would be called *The Second Woman* or *Love After Love*, I really despised myself as I sat there telling Héloise about how Luke still loved his ex-girlfriend but initiated a lot of hugs with me.

When I was finished Héloise said I should ask Luke out, those were her words, Ask him out, as if he was someone who I didn't know at all, a random man who I could ask out to the cinema, someone who I might end up sleeping with just incidentally if we had both had a drink and were both in the mood there in my room. That really depressed me, Ask him out. I felt that I could say I would die for you or I really could die, those were the options, say I would die for you or really just die. I wished I had spoken to Anna instead, she would never have said that, but I couldn't bring the topic up again, I really couldn't.

○

I was walking back from Sainsbury's that night carrying a pack of little Alpro yoghurts and a man shouted at me across the street What would you do to me. I really didn't understand what this man was talking about for a long time, I kept thinking about it the whole time I was walking to my room and eventually it struck me that he was asking something sexual, he was asking what I would do to him in sex. I was so shocked by this, I didn't think men thought of me in that way at all and I especially didn't think that a man would say something like that right in the middle of the street, the whole thing felt very unreal. I didn't even see what the options were, what could I do to that man, I could let myself be fucked by him, I really didn't see what my options were.

Suddenly I remembered a short story I had read, Something That Needs Nothing by Miranda July, and I reread it immediately through the Google Books free sample function. Something That Needs Nothing was a story about two best friends, one of them had always been in love with the other and by the end of the story that friend who was in love had started working in a peep show doing these awful sexual performances for men. Somehow it seemed like when she was doing her peep show persona this potential for love or at least a kind of intimacy was opened up between her and her friend, it created a distance between them which made sexual acts possible, and the girl almost felt that she had something she desperately needed, then. All she wanted was for the two of them to be something that needs nothing together, something like paint on the wall, something complete. But in the end nothing was possible, everything was grounded in something very false and it couldn't be sustained, it couldn't hold.

When I first read this story I had been younger, maybe seventeen, and it had almost creeped me out, I hadn't wanted to know about that peep show. But this time it was perfect, a few times while I was reading the story I almost gasped in amazement and in recognition, it really was an amazing story.

The idea of sex seemed obvious, once I had read it, I couldn't believe I hadn't thought of it myself. Obviously I didn't think that sex would bring about some great transformation, even in Something That Needs Nothing that didn't work, but I did feel that a new dynamic might be triggered by it. I felt that sex was the greatest and most frightening barrier between me and Luke and that a kind of change being provoked around it could be some very positive thing, it could break down a small part of the indestructible wall and create something which did very badly need to be created in order for anything to change or progress. Perhaps sex was a necessary component of the life that I wanted, perhaps some things really couldn't be accessed at all except through sex, like those small boys trapped in that underwater cave who could only be saved by a perfectly shaped and specifically made submarine.

While I was sitting at my desk with Something That Needs Nothing still open on my laptop I set up a Tinder account very rapidly and suddenly without even thinking. Almost without breathing I uploaded photos of myself, a photo of myself dressed as Phoebe Bridgers at Héloïse's Halloween party last year, a photo of me sitting on the outdoor deck of a boat, that was a photo my mother had taken and I was smiling a huge smile in that photo, a smile so huge that it was actually blinding, my eyes screwed very tightly shut.

It was oppressive, the number of men who existed on the app, and all these men could see my photos, the Phoebe Bridgers photo and the huge smile photo. I felt like I hadn't known there were that many men in the world even, it was very strange to me, that unending torrent of men and all of them looking at me. I sat at my desk and looked at endless photos of men with biceps and stupid suits and ties, men who were obsessed with yelling out into the world about their height, 5'11", 6'2", 5'8", 5'9", men whose interests were Netflix, hiking, fun and food, men who said If you want a bad boy I'm bad at everything, men who said I want to fuck you until you are bleeding.

○

Luke was very excited by my idea, he was so tender as I told him about it, he said it was very exciting and that the men who I would meet were extremely lucky and I could feel myself reddening and smiling a delighted, blissful smile, I could feel a warm glow passing between us as Luke told me again and again about those lucky men and by the end I was excited to meet one of the men and to tell Luke about it and for Luke to say again that the man had been so lucky. I really couldn't wait for that conversation about the very lucky man.

Luke told me, then, that Mia had sent him a long message, it was some kind of update message, a general update on her life and thoughts. Luke was very confused and distressed by the message and he hadn't read it completely, it seemed like he'd skimmed it with his eyes half shut. The main part of the message he wanted to discuss was the part where Mia was talking about a famous book she'd read, *A Little Life*. Mia had said the book was about A trauma of the most terrible kind and Luke kept saying Where did she learn to talk like that, he said she had never used phrases like that when they were together and that her use of that language in this context was very aggressive, very alienating and brutal, almost violently brutal.

I understood what Luke meant. It made sense that him and Mia had a shared language between them, a shared way of talking about things and even thinking about them, and it wasn't hard for me to see how the phrase A trauma of the most terrible kind could reject that shared language entirely. Luke and I would never talk like that with one another, I would laugh in his face if he described something as A trauma of the most terrible kind. But at the same time I felt that there was no other way of describing some things. Maybe some things really were traumas of the most terrible kind, maybe those words were just a necessary reflection of reality and not any kind of choice at all. Some things really were very terrible.

○

I started talking to a man called Richard who said he was a comedian. Richard sent voice notes instead of normal texts and he sounded maybe nice, I still assumed everyone weird-seeming was deep down kind and nice. He said I should come over to his flat that week and I said Sure. I said Do you have any pets because I'm a bit allergic, somehow I thought that this question would make me feel safe as if Richard was just some adult I could talk to about allergies and pets, I actually don't know what I thought that question would do. Richard sent me his first typed reply, he wrote No pets unless you count a huge dick. When I told Luke this inside the kitchen he said Jesus, I can't believe he really said that, and I showed him the text, No pets unless you count a huge dick right there and staring out at us, staring out at me alone and daring me to respond. Luke said Are you sure you want to meet this person and I said It actually seems easier to meet someone like this, it seems easier to do something more extreme you know. I think Luke did understand what I meant, he said Ah yes, keep it alienated. And then we looked at each other and laughed over the countertops without actively seeking to construct an atmosphere of alienation.

○

Somehow I felt that I wanted to wear something quite childish and definitely very unsexual to meet Richard, I wanted Richard to feel some kind of pity for me or just a great and overpowering absence of attraction. I wore a huge brown pullover hoodie and huge pair of jeans and my hair looked like the ragged greasy bob of some adolescent skater. I was pleased with that, I did feel protected by that, in that moment I really liked that my appearance was so completely formless.

Richard's flat was not close to my block, it wasn't even in the right city. It was actually hilarious to me that the person I would end up losing my virginity to was this thirty-three-year-old comedian who had warned me about his huge penis and who lived in a flat in some village somewhere not even geographically close to me. It reminded me of the monkey with the randomly moving eyes actually. That monkey's random eyes would land on Richard for sure, he really was that random.

But after days of finding Richard's randomness hilarious suddenly I did become afraid, on the bus to his house I finally did feel fear. As I sat there on the dirty geometric patterned bus seat I felt for the first time that my life wasn't a game and that it wasn't in any way disposable and I suddenly couldn't understand why I had felt that doing this would offer me anything which might hold value. I looked out through the windows at the long blank fields and my face hung there suspended white and freakish. I thought of the Mark Strand poem about how in a field a person is the absence of field. I was the absence of field and the field stretched out around me like a metaphor for something, like a way of talking about being alone.

Richard was waiting at the bus stop, he was the only person waiting and the sight of him standing there gave me an inexplicable orphaned feeling. I wanted him to tell one of his comedian jokes as soon as I got off the bus to somehow change the genre of the situation we were in but he obviously didn't, he said Hi without really smiling and I said Hi with a big friendly smile like I was some kind of patronising TV presenter for children. I really didn't know what mode of behaviour I was supposed to adopt in this situation, I felt that all night I would be alternating between different genres of person because there was no way of acting which felt natural or right, I was completely alone and without landmarks or history. It reminded me of something we had learnt about in anthropology, some civilisations whose monuments had been destroyed by war so that the countries lacked collective history, they almost lacked all memory. Somehow those civilisations felt very relevant to me as I gave Richard a great smile beside the rapidly departing bus.

As we walked to his flat Richard was basically silent which alarmed and even upset me, I felt that he was the adult in the situation and should carry the majority of the conversational burden. I felt very strongly in that moment that Richard hated me and was trying to punish me for something even though I knew that this thought made no sense. Maybe Richard was just someone who wasn't so interested in conversation, maybe he was more focused on the corporeal. I thought about that for a long time as we walked, about that word, corporeal. I had forgotten what its antonym was, I tried for a long time as we walked to remember its antonym but maybe there was no antonym to corporeal.

Once we arrived Richard went to make us tea which surprised and even disturbed me, it felt situationally totally inappropriate. I turned on the TV and it started playing a programme where a man walked through a supermarket in lots of coats and jumpers and knocked items off the shelves with his arms. I couldn't tell what type of programme it was, if it was meant to be funny or somehow informative and cautionary. Richard came back with the tea and sat down next to me. He was quiet for a while and then made an unconvincing kind of comment relating to my body and the fact that he had been thinking about it as we watched the supermarket programme. I started to laugh and then corrected myself and looked away from Richard at the wall behind his bed. I wasn't sure if I was supposed to act serious or unserious or if Richard was being ironic and mocking. I started to laugh again and self-protectively touched my neck. I wondered if it seemed sexual to put my hand on my neck, like an instruction: touch my neck. I guess it did because Richard asked me then if there was anything I wanted to try and I said Sure. Sure was suddenly such a useful word, it really communicated reluctant acquiescence very clearly, without disrupting any predetermined series of events at all. It was a speech act totally free of consequence.

We took our clothes off, then. I carefully placed my clothes in a neat pile beside my backpack so that I could look over at any time and see all my things together in a single visual field. It was so nice to have so many possessions there to ground me, I was lucky to have so many things, to have that whole skater boy outfit and I laughed to myself then, I laughed in my mind at this stupid situation I had constructed for myself, really constructed out of nowhere. I could use my mind and body to create things which felt completely alien to me, some situation where my things were in a pile by the leather sofa of a naked stranger.

I looked over at Richard then and saw that he had a huge tattoo of a coyote's smiling face on his forearm. I was so glad that that coyote was there in that moment, I felt that it added a sinister edge to the situation, some real overtones of predation which were so obvious and explicit that they actually made everything much less frightening. That smiling coyote made everything so stupid and false in that moment, I was very grateful for that. After I thought for a long time about how stupid and false everything was I noticed how long and white

Richard's body was, it was so long, there was so much skin. I could see dark veins all over his penis, it made it look dangerous and electric like some kind of medical experiment. It looked very painful to me actually, I was glad that it wasn't my body.

The first thing Richard wanted to show me was his banjo string, a pink string of skin. He said Be careful, this can snap. He said he knew some guys who had had their banjo strings snapped by girls. I felt that the banjo string was some stupid invention Richard had made up, I really doubted that it had any kind of meaningful existence out there in the world but I said Sure and I promised to be careful because it did seem serious, I didn't want Richard to feel that I might destroy his body, that I might inflict upon him some Trauma of the most terrible kind.

Richard went down on me, then. As he did he said Other guys won't go down on you like this. He said they would be less patient and less giving. He said I might be peaking too early, that after this time I would be disappointed with every guy. These things didn't feel cruel, they didn't feel surprising or even notable, they were just a part of my body's surroundings, part of the unfamiliar sea of input I was surrounded by as I lay on my back there on the bed in Richard's room.

The act felt strange, like an animal licking, an animal with a warm soft mouth that could bite deep into the heart of me without realising it had gone too far and I had broken or torn. It wasn't really nice or bad, it was just full of hot liquids everywhere, Richard's wet spit all over me. I wondered if the way my body stiffened in response meant that I didn't want it or if that was what sex was actually for, for the body to tense up and freeze like that. I started making stupid heavy panting sounds which once they began felt natural and unstoppable and Richard stopped immediately then, stopping with a great proud smile like he had made some huge success of things, like I had undergone my sexual initiation and been reborn. I really hated Richard in that moment, I couldn't bear the idea that he thought of himself as my sexual awakening. That idea nauseated me more than anything he could do to my body would ever nauseate me.

Richard taught me to go down on him then, he just directed my body with his words very clearly and authoritatively like someone teaching me a new kind of sport. It was so easy, it was so similar to how it had felt to eat meat before my parents allowed me to become a vegetarian: you just had to keep it in there and not gag. It even tasted the same. It was nice to know that I could follow instructions with my hands and mouth and make a man come. I had always been good at following instructions but I was still surprised by that. It did mean something quite significant to me, to know that I was able to do that. That knowledge opened up a great array of possibilities to me right in that moment, I could almost see them stretching out ahead of me, stretching out across Richard's mattress.

Richard told me that the next step was sex and I asked if he had condoms. He did, he put one on. He started pushing himself onto my body and in that moment it suddenly seemed implausible that this was what sex was, for a small fraction of a second I really did lie there trying to remember whether this actually was sex or if sex was maybe some other thing. For a much longer time after that I lay there waiting for the moment of transformation, the moment when my body would open itself up and lovingly absorb Richard's, but that moment didn't come, the moment would never come, the moment when my body would decide that it wanted Richard to somehow pierce its skin and enter. So: my body remained closed even when a man was there, expecting things from me, hoping I'd break open. Actually I wasn't surprised by that, I wasn't at all surprised that there had been no unclenching, no welcoming in, I didn't have many feelings about that except that it was quite interesting to me that my body and my mind were synchronised at that very sophisticated level: the level of keeping Richard out of me. My body was reacting like it had its own internal mind, or like it was a kind of computer following a set of instructions which had been entered by a human and which it had to obey because of Asimov's laws of robotics.

Richard didn't seem surprised by what was happening either and he said it would be better if we didn't use a condom, he said the condom created too much friction. I said no and Richard said he was glad I had said no, that he had wanted to give me practice saying no to men. Finally I was shocked, then, shocked by how shamelessly Richard was offering me these false, scheming kindnesses and how totally stupid he thought I was. It was so depressing, that Richard would have let me become pregnant, that I might, in some other life, have had to go to an abortion clinic to actually abort Richard's baby.

Richard got up, then, and stood with his back to me while he pulled up his pants and then his trousers and it was so easy to leave, to walk out into the air and to feel it engulf me. I wanted to undress right there and let the cold fill every crack inside of me. I wanted to swim naked in a foreign sea somewhere, to feel the sea as it flowed into each internal channel and then to walk out onto sand, to lie down on a very clean towel or blanket and eat something natural, some orange, some peach, and be entirely alone, alone for days and days and entirely untraceable. I walked down the hill to the bus stop and imagined the feeling: total aloneness, on and on forever.

○

That night and the whole next day I felt completely fine except for a kind of burning inside my vagina, physically

I felt quite bad but emotionally I really was untouched. Anna came over to my room, I told her all about it and she said That sounds horrible, she said it was a really stupid thing to have done which I agreed with but still, it hadn't been so horrible. I felt that I would never think of some purely corporeal experience as horrible at all. It felt like there were many things that could hurt me very badly but that sex wasn't one of them. Sex was some funny almost whimsical distraction from the more serious problems of the mind and the heart, the body was a funny prop which existed vapidly on the side of those things. That was how it felt to me then, that the physical world was pure exterior, a kind of mask which covered all the hidden bones of life.

I tried to explain some of that feeling to Anna and she said You have to take your body seriously, man. That was a good response, actually, that did make sense to me, because she was right, I hadn't been taking the body seriously at all. I wasn't sure I agreed that it had to be serious but I did feel that Anna understood what I was saying. For some reason then I said Sorry and Anna said No you obviously don't need to be sorry. I felt that I had done something quite bad, after I spoke to Anna, but I wasn't sure why it was bad or who it was bad for, I wasn't sure what kind of apology was necessary.

○

I spent a lot of that day writing a story about the sex with Richard, it was a very factual story, it wasn't metaphorical. I called the story The Virgin and read it out in the literary society the next evening. People felt quite ambivalent about it, some people said that it was powerful and even frightening but then lots of other people said it was implausible, they said the girl's feelings about sex were implausible and her stupidity was implausible too, it was really implausible for example that she wouldn't have known what an aroused penis looked like already. Some girl said she resented the faux naïveté of my story, some girl who was probably younger than me and wearing a sort of tiny velveteen jacket. Somehow it was totally immoral to write about girls who didn't know what an aroused penis looked like, somehow that was totally infantilising and actually offensive.

The part that everyone universally hated was the part about the penis tasting like meat. Everyone said that just wasn't true, they said that nobody would think that, it was too horrible. I hadn't been trying to make something horrible at all, I had never been interested in being creepy or shocking. That was my least favourite type of writing, writing that was so blatantly set up to be horrible and to really alienate you as you sat there reading it. I hadn't been trying to do that at all. The penis really had tasted exactly like meat to me, I hadn't made any kind of choice in describing it like that.

I didn't know how to feel after that meeting. Obviously it was depressing, the fact that my feelings were so unrelatable as to be actually implausible to an entire room of people. But on some totally other level the discussion made me feel full of a sharp burning potential. I hadn't thought the way I felt about things was unusual, I hadn't thought I owned anything that could surprise anyone. There was a lot of myself that I could keep from people, suddenly. There was some great well of secrecy inside me, something untouchable.

○

Finally it was time to have dinner with Luke, he said I want to hear everything immediately, we can't waste any time cooking, let's get takeaway. We ordered dumplings and noodles from the internet, I was so excited for this food, I loved takeaways and especially takeaways I could share with Luke, half of each dish for each of us, already I felt very warm and safe knowing that those bowls of shared food were making their way towards us as we sat on Luke's carpet. Luke didn't even mention the question of how and when I would pay him back for the takeaway and that, too, made me feel so loved and held as I sat there, I said Luke I feel so great sitting here waiting for this takeaway and he laughed then and said Okay, okay, no, stop, tell me everything.

I really did tell him everything, I talked him through each moment of the thing, the bus journey, the banjo string, the condom and its friction, I described all these different objects and actions and spaces to Luke as he sat there with his eyes wide open listening to me. By the end I almost felt that he had been there with me, that the experience had been not mine but some shared thing we had lived through together, some shared dream almost or a shared kind of fantasy, something unreal except to me and Luke for whom it lived inside our brains, it was something we could recall to ourselves and almost make real again if we somehow wanted to, if we somehow decided to do that.

Luke said Wow I have so many thoughts about this and then immediately his phone rang, the food was ready. He ran out of the room to collect it and I sat cross-legged on his floor thinking about what his many thoughts might be, trying to work out what my thoughts would be if I was Luke, I really didn't know. It was very exciting, to be speaking to someone whose thoughts and feelings I couldn't guess at all, and for a moment there I felt that that was love: that total inability to know what someone was going to say and think and feel and the constant wish to know those things, that real desperation to know and understand those things fundamentally and intuitively. That endless and insatiable wish to know things seemed to me at that moment to be the absolute root of love and desire, but when Luke walked back through the door carrying our steaming paper bag of food I knew I'd been completely wrong, that love was something else entirely. If I had an idea of what love was and that idea didn't have Luke's smiling face right at its centre then the idea was stupid, it really meant nothing.

Luke laid out the food on his floor as he was saying Okay, while I was collecting this I organised my thoughts into two discrete topics. He showed me two fingers very theatrically then and tore open the packets of wooden forks and spoons and chopsticks and tossed these implements dramatically into the bowls of food as I just sat there on the carpet watching this whole show with delight and waiting for the topics to be broached. Luke said Are you ready for thought number one and I said Yes and put a whole dumpling into my mouth. I felt the dumpling splitting open and littering my mouth with so many tiny pieces of shredded vegetable, really delicious little salty shreds of vegetable as Luke said Okay, thought one is that you really mustn't feel bad about it not working, that's happened to me loads of times or like the guy version where I just can't get hard and everything's impossible, it happened the first time I tried to have sex and I felt like I would never be able to do it, I think it's just a stress thing, you really mustn't feel bad about that.

Luke and I took a simultaneous bite of the noodles then and with that noodle bite fresh in my mouth I said

Luke thanks for saying that, I mean I guess I actually haven't been feeling bad about it because I wasn't really like aroused so it makes sense. Luke said Aha, this was thought number two. He said I just didn't like listening to that because it seems so obvious that you weren't like enjoying it and I just don't get why you were doing it. He said I don't get why you wouldn't just do the things you want to do and I said But I can't have everything I want just because I want it. I said that while staring very deep into the bowl of noodles and seeing all those hundreds of tiny yellow noodles lying on top of one another, all those hundreds of overlapping little noodles just lying there waiting to be eaten. Suddenly the atmosphere in Luke's room felt completely alien to me, suddenly it felt like there was some frightening thing in the room with us and I didn't know whether to ignore that thing or to provoke it somehow, to really make it scream right there in the centre of Luke's floor, to make it really scream there on the floor like that.

I looked up, then, and Luke was looking straight at me, and it felt like we sat there for a whole minute or more just staring at each other's faces and trying to find some kind of meaning in them, trying to find something legible. Eventually he said I just think the things that should happen will happen you know, I don't think you should be forcing yourself to do anything. I said Thank you, okay, and then I said Can I show you a song.

I typed I Will Mitski into Luke's laptop then and put on the song, it was a song where Mitski was saying that she desperately wants to care for the person she is singing to, to wash their hair and tell them that their feelings are good, it was quite a gentle song until suddenly Mitski is screaming about how all she ever wants is this person who is clearly not listening to her, she's screaming desperately and actually angrily and I could feel myself becoming red and vibrating slightly as I sat there next to Luke listening to it, I could feel my body really shaking as I heard Mitski singing those things as I sat there next to Luke.

Luke 'liked' the song then, he placed it inside his computer without really saying anything and I didn't mind that, I also had nothing to say after that song, everything had been said already and there was relief in that, there was relief in knowing that if Luke was unsure of what I wanted to say then he could open his computer and listen to that song in his Spotify, listen to the words Mitski was singing and the words she was shouting and come to understand some part of something.

Somehow I did actually sleep well that night, somehow I did feel held by Luke as I lay there in my single bed. I imagined him playing the Mitski song from his computer, I imagined him sitting at his desk there in the sink light listening to it. It seemed almost certain to me that that was what he was doing in that moment, as I lay there in my bed inside the dark.

○

The next day all of our lectures were going to be videos, we weren't allowed to go to lecture halls, a great storm was happening and people thought that we might get injured if we left our rooms. Each day life surprised me, it seemed very strange that this was a possibility, our lectures being turned into videos because of weather. I sat in my room and watched a video my psychology lecturer had taken of himself inside his kitchen speaking about memory. How do we remember things? We retrieve them into our minds. I couldn't perceive any kind of storm going on but when I left my room that evening a huge branch was lying in the middle of the road, the branch of a fir tree, I think, just lying amputated there in the road and blocking the road completely. Some machine would come and move that branch tonight, probably, and then the branch would be gone.

○

I got an email from the Careers Service saying I was eligible for a priority careers appointment because I would graduate soon. Somehow this really hadn't occurred to me, this question of jobs and graduation, it was very frightening to be alerted to these things so suddenly, to realise that in four or five months I would need to have some kind of job or some other idea of what I was going to do, what I was going to do for the whole endless rest of my life. Suddenly I saw the whole rest of my life just lying there ahead of me, lying there so blankly and so stupidly. It made me feel very shaky to think about my life like that, to think about that point in time when I would no longer be living in this room beside the kitchen and beside Luke's room too, beside all these things which were themselves my life, which were not separable from life. I thought very suddenly and clearly then that it would be better to die than live in anticipation of that endless time, but it was just a set of words inside my head, that thought, it didn't carry weight and I could destroy it easily as I sat there in my desk chair pulling out so many rough-feeling hair strands, there were endless very rough-feeling hairs on my head that day and it was good to be sitting there pulling them out like that.

I spent that day applying for jobs, I applied for a job as a research assistant and a job curating the Wellcome Collection and a job as a teaching assistant and then I applied to be an editor of the *New York Times*. It was almost reassuring to me, to be sending out all these endless ridiculous applications, and I didn't even tailor my CV to any of the jobs, I sent the same stupid CV each time and I think the CV was a CV I had produced in high school, I think it said that I was a good communicator because I had given a visitor a tour of the school on an open day. It wasn't even true that I had given a visitor a tour. It almost felt true because I had been very afraid of that idea, I had built up a very vivid mental image of the tour I might have had to take that visitor on.

That evening I asked Luke if he had been applying for jobs and it turned out he already had a job. There was a company which did exactly what he was doing in his Master's project, it made fake computer models of objects to somehow help designers make those objects real and so he had a job making more fake computer versions of objects, trapping more things inside computers. The job was going to start in July and it was a work-from-home job so he could live anywhere. Probably he would live with David who had a job in London making computers more intelligent somehow, making their predictions more sensitive. I asked Luke if he would ever want to live with me instead and he said It would be too tiring, we'd be laughing all the time, how would we rest our minds and bodies. Luke phrased things very beautifully when he was trying to be funny, when he was trying to be soft on me and to distract me from meaning through language. I had no answer to his question, How would we rest our minds and bodies. I really didn't know how we would ever be able to do that.

○

That night I replied to a message some boy called Guy had sent me. The message was an incomprehensible joke about weed. I 'loved' the message by clicking on it twice and then I asked Guy if he wanted to come to my room. I met him outside my block less than half an hour later, he was wearing some kind of ugly Hawaiian shirt in a sarcastic way I think and together we walked silently and rapidly back to my room. For some reason Guy thought the first room we passed in the corridor was mine, he turned the doorknob of that room and pushed the door and I just kept walking very quickly without looking back until he understood that the room wasn't mine and caught up with me in the corridor. I didn't see if he had managed to open that door or if the other person had seen him, if they had been afraid or if there had been anyone there at all. I wasn't sure if there had been another person, what they'd seen.

Guy had brought weed with him and we smoked it in my room with all the windows open so we didn't set off the smoke alarm. The rain was pouring through the windows, those slanted windows were a great and unredeemable structural mistake. The weed had no effect on me which didn't surprise me at all and Guy also seemed very cogent, he seemed untouched by the weed too and I wondered if it was fake in some way or if Guy had somehow produced it himself. He told a very long anecdote then about how Princess Diana is important because she exemplifies the cultural obsession with the archetype of the princess who falls from grace. It turned out that this anecdote was somehow his dissertation.

After so many minutes of talking about Princess Diana Guy gestured lazily towards the bed and said Shall we in a very dead dispassionate way. I wondered, in that moment, what it was about me that meant nothing ever happened naturally, nothing was organic and things only happened because a person had forced them to happen through some unbearably crude speech act. Even my own death I would have to beg for, I would have to prostrate myself begging for even my own death.

Guy became naked then and so did I and we were kissing on the bed. If someone had asked me what his body was like I would have had no idea at all, I had no idea if it was hairy or muscular or if his penis was big, I was just randomly kissing at his face as he kissed at my face and neck and tiny speckled nipples. Guy signalled meaningfully towards his penis then, he loved communicating through gesture, and I said Do you have a condom. He said Sure and took one from a little packet in his rucksack, put it on. Then he was shoving his penis at my body so randomly and stupidly, really just shoving his penis at my body like he thought that through persistence he could split me right open, like I would break if I just knew that he wanted me to break. I said Sorry this happens sometimes and Guy said Does it happen every time and

I said Yes, because one out of one was every, one out of one was some eternal number of times.

Guy sighed heavily then and rolled over towards his pants and put them on and then he put on all of his clothes, he was desperate to be clothed suddenly and I really couldn't care less about material things like that in that moment and kept lying there naked on the bed. In Guy's rucksack was a ham sandwich very nastily wrapped up in cling film which he ate while standing up and then he ate an orange which was lying on my bookshelf. He left, then, and I got dressed and changed the sheets and carried the dirty sheets to the washing machine. I watched them there in the washing machine, churning around desperately. I watched the awful condensation which formed on the window of the washing machine.

○

The next day my vagina was stinging again, in the hot kind of way that I imagined a burn would sting. It was so strange to me, that my body could produce so much rootless pain, so much pain inside a totally untouched place. My body could only live in fear of the pain that any real contact would cause. Perhaps even one touch would be too much, one real touch and I would just combust. The whole thing felt very metaphorical, like a complex extended metaphor I had invented myself. If I wrote a story the girl in the story would obviously have an impenetrable skin around her whole body, she would obviously feel some great burning pain whenever a person tried to penetrate that skin, the whole thing felt very obvious to me and very constructed, very cerebral.

There was no reason to do any work on that day. I went to a cafe but everyone in the cafe was standing around solemnly. It turned out that someone who had worked in the cafe had died. A man was describing some series of events in very upsetting detail, he was saying that that person hadn't replied to his WhatsApp messages for days so he had called and called their phone and then called all their next of kin, their husband, their mother, no one answered. Eventually he called the police and the police found that person dead in their bed. It seemed like he really wanted to upset everyone very badly, he was sharing every horrible detail imaginable and some of the details even felt invented, the detail of the police breaking into that person's house and finding the body, that felt very overdramatic. I left the cafe then, I really had no part in that conversation.

○

Somehow I developed the idea that lots of harsh physical exercise would save me, I think it was Luke who planted that idea in my mind, Luke really did believe in the power of exercise. I started going for long runs at night, the idea of anyone seeing me on some daylit run was very humiliating. I ran through the fields behind the city and it was hard, in the dark, to see the paths through the fields, to distinguish between the path and the grass and the mud and even the river, I would be running almost blindly and knowing that at any moment I might encounter some new kind of terrain and fall or be engulfed by some wet frightening thing, I really had to run while being completely aware of that fact.

On Tuesday I started some nauseating heavy period but still went out for one of those awful runs and I actually shat myself there in the field, some wet shit bursting out of me as I ran along an invisible path through the mud. It was almost entirely contained by my sanitary towel but still I had to walk back to my room heavy with the feeling of my own waste right there on my body. I felt that I would surely get some awful infection but I didn't, it was awful in a completely different way to that. It did nothing but still it was very terrible.

The next night I told Luke about the shit but I told him it was a vomit, somehow I felt that the distinctions between holes were very meaningful and that the story was shocking without being overly revolting if it was a vomit. I think Luke was impressed by the vomit story. I felt that he admired the idea of me pushing myself physically, I felt that he thought it would do me good, to be out there in my environment and using my body actively. He never actually said that at all, it was just a feeling I had.

○

I had missed two anthropology lectures that week so I wasn't sure how to approach my next essay, some essay about modernity and the economy. I went to the small and dark psychology library and thought about modernity. Somehow I wasn't interested in reading about it, it felt sufficient to me to just think about it, to really think about modernity. I ended up writing a very random essay about non-fungible tokens, how the idea of the non-fungible token makes economics meaningless because nothing can be traded for anything. Objects had the capacity, now, to destroy chains of transactions forever. I wrote in my essay: The maxim that energy can never be created or destroyed, only transferred, no longer rings true in the economic domain. Then in an appendix I included an example of a non-fungible token: a small cartoon ghost covered in a repeating pattern of the Gucci logo.

Somehow no one in my seminar group had heard of non-fungible tokens, not even the supervisor had heard of them. It seemed like everyone thought that they were something I had invented, everyone nodded very patiently at me as I explained the concept of the non-fungible token. Probably people thought that I had drawn that ghost illustration myself, that I had sat there at my desk patterning that ghost's body with the Gucci logo. But I would never do something like that. I had never been someone who was interested in inventing false facts about the world.

That Saturday I went on a pointless breakfast date with a man called Nick. We met in a cafe on the outskirts of the city on a residential side street near the train station. When I arrived Nick was already waiting there looking like some generic skater, really like the vague impression that somebody might have of what skaters in general looked like rather than like any individual person. It seemed like on every date I went on, one person had to be the skater boy, one person had to be wearing those big jeans and that big hoodie and have that horrible greasy hair hanging all over their face. This time it was Nick's turn, I was wearing a nondescript outfit which was mostly a raincoat.

We sat outside the cafe and drank sour coffees. Nick told me about different celebrities he had met at parties and I had heard of barely any of these celebrities, they were from TV shows about druid battles. I wanted to make some kind of comment about how not everything in the public sphere is of interest to actual specific individuals, how the private sphere is not some perfect microcosm of the public sphere, but I obviously didn't. Instead Nick told me about a theory he'd made up, which was that all people contained a primal violence which modern society didn't let them express. For this reason Nick and his friends often held fights in their living room and hit one another as hard as they could like in *Fight Club*, they gave all of their strength to those fights.

I was almost interested in this idea, I was certainly interested in the idea of repressed and inarticulable urges. That was something very interesting to me. I wondered what made Nick frame this feeling as a special theory he had authored when to me it was a knotted and inexpressible tangle of physical sensations that I would never share with a stranger wearing a raincoat outside some cafe, I would never even dream of doing that. I was suddenly afraid that Nick was making up these violent feelings on purpose, that he thought I might find that seductive, the idea of a man full of primal violent urges. Increasingly men were repulsive to me, increasingly they really were laughable and increasingly Luke was not a man at all: he was so outside of these things, so uninterested in theorising at me, in projecting himself onto anything. Luke would never sit outside some cafe really boring me, without even trying he would be being delightful and hilarious and yet really revelatory, he would be being all those things without trying to perform them at all.

Nick told me about how he loved the writer Mishima. He loved the violence in Mishima's novels. He loved the scene in one of Mishima's novels in which some boys killed a cat or popped a cat's eyeball or some brutal act like that. I had actually read a book by Mishima but I wasn't interested in talking about that, I was happy to let Nick speak and to feel that he had something new to teach me about literature and violence. He really did like talking about that scene with the cat's eyeball, it almost felt like he had wanted to go on a date purely so that he had some new person to talk to about the ruined eyeball of that cat.

Less than half an hour after the date ended, Nick texted me saying that he would love to see me again. It was so easy to make men crave my company: I just had to say nothing and keep my clothes on and sit there stupidly in some raincoat. It was actually really depressing, that Nick wanted to see me again. It was really depressing that Nick wanted to date me and that Luke, with whom I was so funny and so giving and so totally alive, somehow didn't at all. That fact seemed extremely cruel.

○

I started going to lectures again, they were fascinating to me suddenly, way more fascinating than I remembered them being: it was obviously much better to be going to lectures and thinking about things than to be going for horrible runs. I went to a lecture on the discovery of the human womb. A man called Vesalius had cut open the womb of a woman who had been sentenced to death for an unknown crime, and he had seen a small corpse inside her body. Thus the womb was discovered. So many other men had been there also, all these men with pointed beards wearing some kinds of caps or bonnets on their heads. All you could see of the woman was her stupid cone-shaped breasts and then the dark pit of stomach which some man was reaching into, his thin white hand hanging above that pit filled with intestine and dead baby.

After this lecture I had written an essay on anatomy as gendered violence and surprisingly my supervisor loved this essay, he said it betrayed a dark view of the world which was in fact accurately grounded in a rich understanding of women's sixteenth-century social realities. This comment was extremely invigorating to me, it made me feel like I understood something I hadn't thought I understood at all. Maybe I understood a lot about the structure of the world just through some unarticulated feeling that I had within my body. Maybe I was producing a dark and accurately grounded view of the world right at that moment just through living.

○

I told Luke about my date with Nick and he said, You should be feeling very sorry for yourself with all these dates, we should give ourselves a treat. Then immediately we spent a very whimsical afternoon together, that was the treat. We walked along the river to a forest neither of us had known existed, and found an old rope swing just hanging there. We took turns on the swing, standing on the mound of knotted rope as we glided over little piles of leaves and the heavy earth beneath them. Luke pushed me and it was unlike any other feeling, swinging and knowing I'd return at any moment to the feeling of his palm against my back, his fingers resting for a second in the dent beside my spine and then pushing me away, with both of us knowing that in pushing me away he was also sending me back, gliding back over the ground towards his hands. I could have gone back and forth for hours, really hours, I could have gone back and forth forever, on and on forever.

We walked around another part of the forest then, a man-made part filled with clay caverns. We passed a woman and many children who asked us if we knew the way out, but we didn't. I said Sorry, I have actually never been here before. But when we decided to leave we found our way immediately, emerging onto a hillside looking out over the city. For some reason we decided to roll down the hill, one after the other. Luke rolled first and I stood there and watched him roll away. Then we swapped and he watched me roll into the distance, my glasses falling from my face into the grass as I rolled. I called up to him from the bottom of the hill without seeing him, seeing only an anonymous figure standing above me on the hillside. I had trusted that I knew and loved that figure, and shouted up to him some exclamation of real joy.

Luke and I had filmed each other rolling down the hill but when I got back to my room and was alone again I deleted those films. Somehow they reminded me of some very pressing future in which he would leave me to go rest his mind and body. I could so vividly imagine some future time in which I would be entirely alone and watching those films of Luke rolling away into the distance, rolling away and descending, there, into something unrecognisable, something almost imperceptible, just a grey line at the bottom of a hill. That would be all that I had left of Luke: a video of him getting further and further away from me.

○

The next day I watched a Žižek programme on my laptop. The programme was much more emotional than I expected, it wasn't at all abstract. Žižek talked about anxiety, he said that anxiety is the only honest emotion, that all other emotions are a trick. Then he showed a clip from *The Birds* where a woman discovers a man's body mauled by birds and starts to scream in a frightening silent way. Then Žižek says that anxiety is silent, see, she cannot even scream.

Suddenly that week I was surrounded by frightening animal things, it was like that film clip had triggered a response from my environment and made it very interested in frightening me through the bodies of animals. While I was walking in the fields behind my block a squirrel jumped down from a tree and latched itself onto my leg, clinging with its claws tearing through my jeans and scraping at the surface of my skin. I was so afraid to touch that squirrel and yet I did reach down and wrap my fingers round its squirming stomach, I really had to pull at the squirrel and I felt that I might burst it but eventually it did fall away. As it fell I saw a fleshy webbing form between its legs and body, some webbing designed to slow down its fall. I hadn't known that squirrels were webbed in that way. Then as I was crossing the road back towards my room I saw a badger run from the greenery on the side of the road into the road, stand in the road, and be killed.

○

I sent Luke a song called The Place Where He Inserted the Blade by this band Black Country, New Road. It was a strange multipart song which started with this quiet piano and then built up to a great crashing finale which went on for four or five minutes, some very intense heavy section where a man is shouting about how whenever he tries to make lunch or use his soup maker he is reminded again of this person he is singing to, he is shouting Show me where to tie the other end of this chain as if there's some great chain hanging from him and tying him to this person but it isn't attached to their body at all, he is tied in place to nothing and he is shouting The rest of my body is yours now to no one. It was a very depressing song but one I thought that Luke would like, and the part about the soup maker and all the food smells that came out of it, the chicken and the broccoli, was funny and strange in a way that felt like something Luke had invented himself.

I think he did like the song, he sent back a gif of a dark pit as if to say that the song spoke to a dark pit inside him but then he sent me some beepy electronic song, some upbeat wordless electronic song like the looping soundtrack to a children's video game, the soundtrack to Pac-Man. It felt very aggressive, that Luke would send me such an emotionless song; it felt to me that the song was him saying You make me feel nothing. I listened to it the whole way through in case it contained some great rich secret at its end but of course there was no secret and I turned the music off then and just lay there in my bed with no sounds playing. That felt very Žižekian, the production of that great anxious silence.

I found a new favourite library that week, it was a library meant for postgraduate law students but no one was policing that and the library was always deserted. It was a huge glass building with a pit inside its centre, some alarming deep drop down into a darkened core in which old law books were stored. The library was full of vending machines including a coffee vending machine which made horrible coffees in really nice little recycled brown cups. There was a fire escape beside the library and I went and sat out there so many times that week, drinking one of the vending machine coffees and looking down at the pavement so far beneath me, all the trees which lined that strip of pavement. I could see them through the metal grating of the balcony or I could lean over the ledge and see them whole and unobstructed, I could see them loose and in their fundamental form as I drank my horrible coffee from the nice little cardboard cup.

We had an anthropology lecture on suicide that week. I was quite shocked that this was something the university would choose as a relevant and enriching lecture topic but the lecture was gripping. Instead of suicide being an individual pathology or tragedy, the lecture said, it could be seen as a kind of protest, or as a way of probing at the self-other boundary in cultures where people are seen as fundamentally enmeshed. If I can kill myself while others live then I must hold some kind of independent body, a body which is mine alone. That was how I interpreted the lecture, I really felt that it was a dangerous lecture, I felt that it positioned suicide as a very logical solution to not even pain but simply dilemmas around selfhood, around the limits of the self. It was dangerous for sure but it really was gripping, to sit there on the fire escape thinking about how much sense it made to try and obliterate one's body when the limits of one's own specific self were in question.

○

I went home that weekend because my family had moved to the new house, now I could see it, it was ours. Somehow on that weekend any house could only speak of loss to me, any house was the site of an imagined but aborted future. My bedroom felt like some place in which Luke and I had lain beside each other and slept every night for some immeasurable amount of time, the kitchen was a place in which one of us had sat at the little white table while the other had cooked something on the stove with gentle music playing and dim evening light streaming in through the windows. It felt like something which had happened an infinite number of times, every night for the whole length of both our lives. The coffee pot on the stove made me especially depressed, like a relic of a life which had been mine and Luke's and which now wasn't and would never be. Me and Luke would have loved to make coffee together in a coffee pot inside a kitchen. I couldn't understand how this house was for my family, I really couldn't connect with it on that level.

There was some kind of industrial physics park beside the house. I had expected that any industrial park would be disused and archaic but this industrial park was filled with active machinery. There was a huge turning wheel with a function I couldn't even guess or google, I didn't know how to describe that wheel to Google. Nothing came out of the wheel, no smoke, no noise, it just stood there turning endlessly in the centre of the park. I guess it was producing something. Then there was a long row of warehouses with signs saying the temperature inside them was subzero, they were ice warehouses.

The industrial park felt like a place out of some movie where somebody would go to disappear amidst a foreign landscape of machines. The industrial park did speak to me. It seemed to me to be a monument to the insatiable and hopeless quest for knowledge of the world, real knowledge which could be gained by using incomprehensible soundless machines. I was glad I had reread some part of *The Catcher in the Rye* then, I was thinking of the way that Holden felt like he would disappear each time he crossed the street. That was how I felt as well as I walked beneath the machines, and Holden didn't seem so alien to me then.

○

For some reason once I got back to college Luke was very interested in talking about how I would feel if he died, if he was murdered right in front of my eyes, on the street or in the kitchen, on the kitchen floor. I actually loved this conversation, I felt it opened up a unique space for a kind of deathly honesty, I could say My life would be ruined, my life would be ruined forever while looking him straight in the eyes and laughing as he laughed back at me with his eyes very firmly fixed on mine. Luke said he thought that I would rend, he said It means to rip up all your clothes in despair and I didn't believe him, I kept shouting Google it Google it and he did. There were very few search results for Rend, lots of the search results were poems and Luke said It's a very literary word. I said Yes, I would rend, and I mimed rending. It was easy to imagine: me, standing in the street and ripping all my clothes up in despair. It was so easy to imagine that I almost felt it must have already happened.

○

On Thursday I went on a new date with Nick, we went to a pub. Somehow Nick had assumed that I would want to have five or six drinks there, he was really confused when I said I only wanted one, genuinely thrown and disappointed by that. We negotiated this for maybe twenty minutes and then Nick used his phone to show me a story he had written. The story was about a boy seeing his pet chicken lying dead in his back garden. Then the boy went to school and punched another boy in the face. The chicken thing had turned him into a bully! It was a terrible story, even just grammatically it was terrible. Nick wanted my feedback, he was really unsatisfied when I just kept saying I like it I like it, obviously he could tell that I was lying and I did feel bad about that. I just felt that if any situation required some awful honesty to be dragged out of me it wasn't this one at all. I didn't need to waste the unbearable pain of speaking some unspeakable truth on Nick's stupid chicken story.

After that drink we went to the house Nick shared with three other men. Nick's housemates were all eating some kind of pork ready meal at the kitchen table. There were so many of those cellophaney ready-meal lids lying around, small sheets of cellophane covered in food juices. For some reason I held my breath as we walked through that kitchen. We reached Nick's room and he pushed the door open. We were stuck inside his room in the dark, then, with only the black sky visible through the windows.

When Nick turned on the lights I saw that his room was endlessly depressing. It was a tiny attic room with very low ceilings and his dirty stuff lying around everywhere, dirty clothes all over the bed. There were black-and-white photocopies of Francis Bacon paintings on the walls and Nick told a long story then about Francis Bacon and a suicide which was somehow linked with a horrible painting of a man on the toilet and a great evil shadow and small scrap of paper in the foreground of the painting. Francis Bacon's work always really scared me so that in that moment I was simultaneously frightened and bored. That had always been my least favourite combination of emotions, I remember thinking that about the Indiana Jones movies as a child: they were terrible to me because they were so scary but also so boring. I really didn't care about what happened to Indiana Jones but at the same time I didn't want some skeleton to jump out from nowhere or a gun to be fired in some man's face. That endless disinterest combined with a real very basic fear was exactly what I was feeling in that moment surrounded by Nick's Francis Bacon photocopies in his tiny dirty room.

Eventually Nick put on a Chinese art movie full of brightly coloured lights and women wearing little corsets, I think it was a film about sex work but it was hard to tell because the subtitles were too small to read on his computer screen. I think he thought this film would create some erotic atmosphere between us, all those bright lights, all those corsets, and Nick started taking off his T-shirt and his trousers. Just like with Guy I didn't see his body at all, I really couldn't have described it to anyone. I didn't feel like taking my T-shirt off and just pulled down my jeans and knickers and lay there underneath Nick looking diagonally upwards at the neon-lit corridor that was visible there in the movie on his computer.

I hadn't bothered asking Nick to use a condom because I knew that he would end up just stupidly pushing his penis against some vague dent in my body, I knew there was no point and I was right, there really was no point at all. His reaction to the situation was unprecedented: unlike Richard or Guy he didn't stop but started pretending we were having some very passionate porn type of sex anyway, slapping at my butt cheeks actually very harshly while at the same time trying to shove his penis inside of me and not even aiming for the right place at all, aiming almost for the hole through which I peed, but I was grateful for the slapping, I did prefer that sharp slap of Nick's palm against my skin to the feeling of nothing in that moment. That slapping really took me out of myself. No one had ever hit me before.

On the way back to my room I phoned Luke even though I was sure he'd be asleep. In fact he answered the call almost immediately. I told him about Nick and the chicken story and the stupid slapping, I didn't think it had upset me but I was crying into the phone then as I crossed some unlit park beside so many invisible bushes and flowers. As I cried there in the park and surrounded on all sides by unseen things I was imagining Luke in his dark room listening, maybe even listening through headphones, my crying wired straight into his brain. I didn't feel that he really understood what I was saying, I didn't think he had ever had a completely horrible sexual experience, but that was almost better: feeling Luke listening to something that he couldn't understand but trying anyway, trying very hard from his bedroom in the dark. That was very beautiful to me.

○

The next morning quite early Luke knocked on my door and said Are you okay but he seemed almost angry. He stepped inside and said Are you sure you want to be having this kind of sex. That made me cry almost immediately, who had ever said that I wanted to be having this kind of sex, of course I desperately didn't. In a cold and hollow way he said I just don't understand why you're putting yourself in these situations. I don't know why I'm putting myself in these situations either Luke I said in an also rough and alien tone of voice. I didn't understand what kind of conversation we were suddenly inside of, I didn't understand what we were doing with all these harsh and actually painful tones of voice but it felt like I had to comply, I had to operate within the conversational limits Luke had established. Luke said Well maybe think a bit more before you just do things and then he left, he really had come into my room just to say those things to me and to turn me into some stupid incomprehensible person inflicting pain upon myself and upon others really indiscriminately and crazily.

I spent the rest of that morning just perceiving the burning in my vagina, really just experiencing that internal burning feeling and hoping I didn't start to need the toilet because I didn't want to engage with any kind of hole ever again. Swivelling in endless circles in my desk chair, I made that burning feeling spin around through pointless circles in my bedroom.

Finally then after hours of me sitting there Luke messaged me, he said I'm sorry if I put too fine a point on it earlier, can we talk about it some more tonight maybe? That was a very classic thing for Luke to say in some situation like this, I could guess what he meant but I wasn't familiar with the phrase To put too fine a point on it, I had to google that and found the example sentence I apologize, I was angry and – not to put too fine a point on it – a little bit drunk when I said those things. I found the example sentence Not to put too fine a point on it, but she said that you sexually assaulted her and then I found the sentence We are dealing with people who are, not to put too fine a point on it, insane. It turned out that the phrase came from *Bleak House* and that *Bleak House* was about a family who waited unsuccessfully to inherit some money. In *Bleak House*, Google said, Passion is both important and dangerous, sometimes healthy and satisfying, sometimes harmful and dangerous. I read all these uninteresting things before I really thought about the meaning of Luke's text and then I wrote back Yes please, then turned my phone off and lay down on top of the duvet of my bed.

○

Luke and I went for a drink that night, we met at the pub rather than walking there together for some reason. The pub was almost entirely empty and filled with dangling strings of lights suspended above every surface, somehow those lights really did shift the atmosphere between us as we stood there waiting to order and I almost reached for Luke's hand then, I almost reached out to touch him.

As soon as we sat down Luke said I'm worried I'm somehow making you feel like you need to have all this sex you're not enjoying. I said How would you be making me feel that and he said I don't know. He said You know you do deserve to do things you like and then suddenly and almost inaudibly he said I care about you so much, you know that. I had to work to keep from crying then and

I was saying Luke I love you and Luke was looking in my eyes then and he wasn't looking away, and beneath the table his knee was moving almost imperceptibly towards the fabric of my jeans and creating some almost imperceptible friction there between those two pieces of denim.

We talked for hours very randomly then about disconnected things like Luke's sister being a fussy eater and crying in a restaurant once because there had been nothing on the menu that she wanted. We talked about a time when my brother was a toddler and had run into the road and both of my parents had screamed, my mum's scream normal and my dad's a horrible low groan. We talked about how Mia hadn't liked some statues in Luke's hometown, statues which stood around a lake in which a man's dead body had been found last year. Somehow we discussed countless situations like this until the pub was closed, with that almost imperceptible friction still alive between our knees.

○

That evening as soon as Luke and I had said goodnight I started touching myself, I was standing up and fell onto the bed with a great shock. I was touching myself even as I fell and I lay there for a long time sending waves of shock all through my body, the waves kept coming, endless spasms flooding through me, I must have come about ten times in a row because each time I reached a peak there was some new peak ahead of me. I was drifting back and forth between myself and Luke as I lay there: I was myself seeing Luke across the table, feeling his thigh hovering softly beside mine, and then I was Luke, hearing myself saying I love you I love you, and in the fantasy of me as Luke it really split me open to hear those words. I was Luke, then, touching myself to the memory of me saying I love you, I was Luke coming and coming to the fact that I loved him, really touching himself with so much feeling and intensity as he played and replayed that memory there in the sink light. For a moment then I lost all orientation, for a moment I was genuinely stranded and not at all sure of who I was and what type of body I was touching. Suddenly it felt like me and Luke were completely interchangeable and living the same fantasy right at that moment, like we existed in our separate rooms but were mentally inhabiting some far more real space in which we were bursting into each other and destroying the limits of each other's separate selves forever.

I took my clothes off then and stood in front of my mirror, seeing my body first as mine and then as some girl's body, seeing my body as Luke might see it, as a body I could fuck with my own body. Neither version seemed more real or persuasive than the other in that moment, both felt plausible but neither was definitive. I lay down and reached into myself then and felt I was split open, I could plunge myself right into me and spread my fingers like a jellyfish pumping itself through water and really push at my own walls without any resistance at all, without pain, even. I lay there for a long time, pushing at my own endlessly penetrable walls.

○

The next day I felt completely weightless and went for a long walk by the river wearing only linen shorts and a T-shirt which said History above a drawing of a figure dancing on a coffin, I don't know where I got that T-shirt, I don't know what it meant. I bought myself a flat white and a pastel de nata from a van and for some reason the person working in the van thought I had ordered two flat whites and no pastel de nata but I didn't care at all, I drank both flat whites at manic speed and shivered, looking straight down into the black water of the river from the iron bridge which joined two screaming roads together. Then when I got back to my room I threw up in the sink. I didn't know how to interpret that vomit, my body was speaking some unreadable language at that moment.

I had asked Luke if he wanted to have dinner and he hadn't opened the text but when I bumped into him in the corridor we went wordlessly together to his room. Once we were inside he said You can sleep here if you want, on the mattress I mean. He meant the spare mattress which lived beneath his bed in a mattress-shaped drawer, I had the same drawer in my room. We pulled the mattress out from its drawer and laid it down there on the carpet by Luke's bed. I went to change into pyjamas and collect my pillows and duvet as Luke kept his door open, his open door leading right out to the hallway. I returned completely drowning in soft things to Luke wearing his pyjama shorts and a T-shirt that said Wikipedia as I stood there wearing that History T-shirt as a kind of dress with tiny dark green knickers on beneath it.

We stayed up for a long time talking, then. Luke told me how he had lost his virginity, he said It sounds impossible but I swear it was in the bathroom of a train station. I couldn't believe we hadn't talked about this before but somehow we really hadn't, I had no mental image of Luke losing his virginity in the bathroom of a train station. I wondered if that was the time it hadn't worked or if he was defining the first time as the first real time, the one I still had ahead of me, and if that was why he was telling me that story: to hint in some vague way at that future time lying there waiting for me, just lying there in the unspeakable future. That first time was with us in Luke's room, then, drifting between us as we breathed in and out into the air inside his room.

We talked, then, about a painting Luke had done in primary school. He couldn't remember what the painting had been of, he just remembered that he'd been so afraid for his parents to see it. He had tried to hide the painting but somehow he had failed. Why was Luke so afraid? He said that he was such a fearful child, not an anxious child but a genuinely fearful one: he had feared a great and unnameable loss that now he couldn't understand, he couldn't touch that feeling.

We stopped talking after that and just lay there with the light on with me looking up at Luke, at his long pale legs stretched out on top of his duvet as he looked down at me with my legs also bare and extended, also littered with endless tiny freckles which could be arranged into any number of patterns. Just like stars those freckles could be said to look like anything, a chained maiden, a bird of paradise, they could be said to be anything because really they were nothing. I almost didn't want to look at Luke, I almost had to force myself to look at him. Somehow I felt within some animal place inside my body that I didn't know what I would do if I saw him lying on the bed. The thing that I would do would be a terrible thing I had invented myself, a second original sin almost, and I said Could you turn the light off please. I sounded weirdly cold when I said that, weirdly cut off from something.

Once it was dark I could hear Luke breathing, I could hear him turning over and I wasn't sure if he was turning towards or away from me. Eventually he said You know

I'm really sorry about everything. I could hear from his voice that he had turned away, he was looking at the wall. Luke was silent then, I think he was asleep. I lay there for hours, looking at the shadow of his shoulder which was visible against the wall. I didn't know how long that shadow would stay visible but in the end it stayed visible all night. If I had stayed on that mattress forever and Luke had stayed on top of his bed and turned away from me I would have lived forever seeing his shadow.

○

The next morning Luke said I feel like you didn't really sleep and I said Oh did I keep you awake, I'm so sorry. Luke didn't respond to this question at all, he said Hey I've got a lecture this morning, do you mind like and I said Of course and folded my duvet very quickly into some great heavy pile and dragged the pile back to my room. I had thought that Luke might see me leaving carrying some huge unsustainable pile of duvet and pillow in some indecent T-shirt and call me back in, call me back and say I'm sorry or Stay with me or even My lecture doesn't start till ten but he didn't, he watched me leave and let me. He had no idea what might happen to me, that was the thought I had right then. Somehow in that moment it really felt terrible that Luke didn't feel some innate drive to protect me. It wasn't the sort of thought I normally had at all, the thought that I wanted protection. I don't even know what sort of threat my brain was thinking of, what threat it was picturing.

I sat on the floor for a long time that morning. There was obviously some endless mass of things to think about, Luke's weird invitation to sleep on his floor, his dark apology, I was surrounded by so many unsolvable problems that I couldn't think at all, I couldn't arrange anything into any kind of pattern or structure. That had always been something I was good at: finding patterns and creating structure. Suddenly life had lost its shape, events had no coherence. It felt like the things that had happened between me and Luke could be arranged in any order, everything would be just as unreadable. I would never be able to talk or even write about it, everyone would criticise what I wrote, they would find it so incoherent and so stupid, just endless random things happening on and on forever without bringing anyone closer to anything. Neither art nor science could save me, there was no meaning to things and no truth either. That was some terrible place to be, that place with no meaning and no truth.

○

I started analysing the data for my dissertation, that felt like a task I could do even without being able to think, I just had to type some numbers into a computer and make the computer reorganise them into a second set of less organic, more manipulated numbers. I still hadn't come to understand computers, to understand their appeal. Really they seemed stupid to me and even dull, they still seemed very limited. I sat at my desk for the rest of that day, typing in numbers to the computer's dumb mind, and I discovered that I had found nothing in my dissertation. Babies who touched more objects were not better at speaking, they were not better or worse, they were the same.

It didn't matter that I had found nothing, my supervisor had been clear that we wouldn't be penalised for that. I think she had known I would find nothing, I think she had found nothing as well. There were very few relationships in psychology: this was something our lecturers often said. In the end very few things were connected to each other.

○

I bumped into Luke in the kitchen the next night and he told me about a problem his friend David was having. David had been dating this girl Lara, but he hadn't really loved her and had found the relationship very taxing in some way, so he had ended it, but him and Lara had stayed friends. Then suddenly last week Lara had said that she couldn't continue the friendship because she was still in love with David. So now he was alone, but there was nothing he could do to change the situation, because he didn't love Lara and would rather never see her again than be her boyfriend.

This story was incredibly depressing to me. At some point in the past David and Lara had not yet known they would look back and see the things that had happened with depressing clarity, see that all along they had been heading towards some great fall.

Suddenly then with a harsh intake of breath I felt I understood why Luke had told me this story, it was a kind of test or some awful callous warning and possibly it wasn't even true, possibly Luke had created it in his own mind or maybe he and David had concocted it together, I could actually imagine that. I said Luke I really have no opinion on this situation and I left the kitchen without even doing anything in it. I actually slammed the door and it made the same sound as Luke's old heartbeat impression, the same dark heavy thudding.

○

Maybe an hour later Luke knocked on my door and even before I opened the door I felt a frightening atmosphere building, a harsh cold charge running between us. He came in and sat down in the desk chair and immediately I said Why are you so angry with me. Luke said Jesus

Christ see this is exactly what I wanted to talk about. I said What do you mean and he said Is it me or has our friendship become ridiculously intense. The way that he said this was like the word intense had some hidden meaning that was too awful to even articulate, some secret deathly meaning and I started crying then. I didn't see why I had to try and hide it, I almost wanted to see what Luke would do to me. Luke said See this is what I mean, I just don't understand why me saying that would make you cry, it makes it really hard to have a conversation, to be honest it's really stressful for me. I said Luke this is very stressful to me too, it's extremely difficult for me and he said Jesus Christ again. I had never heard him use that phrase before and it seemed like he had made a decision to try and alienate me by constructing some random inauthentic dynamic in which he said Jesus Christ and sighed excessively in response to everything I said. He was constructing this dynamic effortfully and painstakingly and forcing me to inhabit it in order to destroy something significant forever, to take something essential out from inside of me and to kill it right there in front of me.

Luke softened slightly as I sat there on the floor wiping the liquids which were streaming out from every hole in my face and streaking my sleeves and he said Look would you ever want to do something more structured, like some other activity together. I said What do you mean, like not dinner? and Luke said I don't know yeah maybe something with some other people too. This made me cry even more and I could feel Luke closing himself off from me again, I had crossed another line, Luke didn't want to be alone with me inside a room but all I wanted was to be alone with him. That was the only thing I wanted so I wasn't making this conversation easy for him, and he wanted to punish me for that.

For no reason at all then he said, You aren't very interested in things, are you. I really had no idea what he meant by this, it just seemed like some random accusation intended to push himself as far away from me as possible. It meant nothing to say that I wasn't interested in things. Our situation wasn't about things, every thing in the world could go away and die and the situation would remain exactly the same, drifting desperately somewhere outside the material world. I almost hated Luke in that moment, I hated the way he said these random meaningless things whenever I felt closest to death. I could feel death right beside me as Luke sat there moving away from me and pushing me from him. And he could sense it when I felt that pull towards death, he could always sense it and he chose to respond with impenetrable comments that pushed me further outside the world, away from any semblance of meaning. He wanted to leave me without landmarks, he wanted to make me feel like my perceptions were completely false and baseless, like I was living in some invented reality that no one would ever understand or sympathise with and that he specifically would never share, he would rather kill me than share that reality with me.

I said Luke can you please go and he did, he left easily and passively as if this was some kind of real ending, an ending so final that he didn't need to be gentle about it, to soften things or to make anything redeemable. I stayed there on the floor, biting hard into my hand and arm and leaving frightening teeth marks all over my skin as if something had come and sunk itself into me, something which wanted very badly to destroy me. It was a really melodramatic thing to be doing, it was as if I was trying to confirm Luke's sense that I was some dangerously intense person and I wondered if that was why I was doing it, if I was harming my body out of a metacognitive impulse to destroy myself in a more deeply psychological way. But I really didn't care about questions like that anymore.

○

It was the Easter holidays, then. I remembered the start of the last holiday. Luke and I had gone out for breakfast and had promised to keep calling each other and we did call each other almost every day as we walked around in the winter air. Every place in my hometown now was a place I had walked through as I opened myself up to Luke, every river, every lake. The next holiday stretched out ahead completely meaningless, so blank and desolate beside that industrial park with its silent machines. I closed my eyes and I saw death, guns being slipped inside of mouths, jumps off of buildings onto empty granite streets, I pictured those things involuntarily but I didn't turn off the thoughts. It was very easy to see those things, to see a gun firing through the roof of a mouth. I didn't even know where my brain had found those images, I had always left the room during violent scenes in movies. My brain was just inventing them from nowhere.

On the car journey home I pretended to be deeply asleep. There were tears streaming down my cheeks and in my fake sleep I couldn't wipe the tears, I let them roll until they reached the neck of my jumper and were slowly absorbed. I saw nothing but I could tell that it was sunny through the red and veiny lids of both my eyes. There was no way to block off my vision. I would be seeing the world for as long as I lived.

○

It was hard to be living in a house with other people in it, it made me realise it had been a long time since I had properly spoken to anyone who wasn't Luke or some man. Almost any conversation topic was upsetting to me, but even when I didn't feel cognitively upset I would often start crying anyway. Me and my brother tried to make some jokes together over dinner. In the past we had made up a joke about how poignant the conditional perfect tense was, we had watched the movie *Aladdin* and my brother had paraphrased a line using the conditional perfect tense, he had said I would have wanted to show you the world. We had laughed, then, about how sad that tense made any sentence sound, and the joke had become associated with the image of an intelligent monkey who had experienced some great loss and was mourning the potential that had once existed: the potential to have been able to show someone the world. Me and my brother had laughed about this for years, but this time when he said I would have wanted to show you the world I was immediately in tears, almost gasping for air at the dinner table. I would have wanted to show you the world: the sentence spoke to me on some unbearably fundamental level and my brother was annoyed, then, our joke was obviously ruined.

In the end I made up a false reason why I was feeling so bad, I told a long story about a boyfriend who had cheated on me and then dumped me, and who had never loved me even though I loved him very much and gave him everything. The boyfriend was called Nick, I guess the boyfriend actually was Nick, that was a little joke I gave myself, a pointless sort of treat, the idea of Nick being able to destroy me. I don't think the story clarified things to my family, no one understood why I hadn't told them about the boyfriend already or why I was so upset about this clearly very brief relationship, the whole story was quite unconvincing but my feelings and my objective reality had become so completely alienated that lying was my only means of accurately expressing myself. But I didn't even know what kind of situation would legitimise my feelings. Only some very horrible situation, only some Trauma of the most terrible kind.

○

My brother was going to study at a distant coastal university so we went to visit a town near the campus and stayed in an awful Airbnb with Union Jack-patterned duvet covers and prints of vintage cars with corny round bonnets everywhere. The town was mainly a long strip of shops and the shops were called things like Beach Treats written in Times New Roman, or they were pleasure arcades called things like Heaven or Flamingo Palace or Flamingo Dreamland. That was the nice part of town. Behind those shops was a second strip of shops: endless shops for repairing faulty phones and a decrepit and smashed-up Poundland. I think everyone was disappointed: we had been told that the town would be full of art and beauty, or we had just believed that for no reason, randomly. Really the world was so unbearably full of horrible things.

We walked along the beach in the wind. We walked along a pier. The pier had an upstairs section, a long elevated walkway with low stone walls. I walked along that walkway and looked over the edge into the hungry-looking dark brown ocean, crashing again and again against the granite of the pier like a computer-generated thing with repeated and identical waves. I climbed onto the roof of some building leading off from the pier, covered in the same dark speckled granite. It didn't look or feel different to be on the roof of that building, it felt the same as being on the ground. Changing one's vantage point really did nothing.

There was a sort of shell-encrusted grotto in that town, that was some other place we went to. It was endless dark tunnels with shells pressed into their walls. That was meant to be impressive, that some people had pushed shells into the fabric of the wall. The shell grotto felt like the setting of a nightmare I might have about the inside of my body: endless dark tunnels leading nowhere with sharp grating walls. There was one room with an ancient photograph of a séance as its wallpaper, crowds of Victorian women standing around in weird fur hats conducting a séance in the grotto. Whoever had made that shell grotto had blatantly designed it to be creepy, which seemed desperate. It seemed pathetic.

○

I was glad to be home from that holiday, back in some unfamiliar house and able to study endlessly. I had learnt everything that I was going to learn from university, now I just had to store it in my mind in an easily retrievable and logically organised way. That was easy to me, I had always been good at controlling memory. I was so good at studying that I could even study while crying. I could separate my mind into two halves and be studying with one half while crying with the other and composing endless messages to Luke with completely different meanings and consequences. Finally I understood what he had meant about the Touch your pussy mode of being: suddenly it felt like there were endless different modes one could inhabit, and each of them created a different reality. Things were impossibly dark and heavy but there was an equally plausible reality in which nothing bad or serious had happened at all, and nothing mattered. I couldn't write to Luke, something unbridgeable had opened up between us, some great phenomenological chasm.

○

I went to the industrial park one night and walked around in it. So many machines were still active even at night, so many machines were still silently moving. The great wheel was rotating endlessly in the centre of the park.

I walked out to the wheel and touched its cold metal body as it moved slowly away from me. I wondered what would happen if I really exerted effort trying to shift the movement of the wheel, if I pushed down hard or climbed up onto it. But the question wasn't interesting to me. I had wanted there to be some kind of telescope in that industrial park, something for seeing things instead of just endlessly producing them. That would have meant something to me.

I stayed away from the ice warehouses. They reminded me of Holden walking around that dark lake with all the chunks of ice stuck in his hair and with nothing but fear for his future. Had Holden wanted to die, then? I don't think the book said. It was so strange, the points in books when people died. Like in The Dead by James Joyce, that man died just from standing outside some woman's house and singing to her through the windows which she couldn't even see out of because they were so wet. As if it was so easy to die. But that man was very delicate, I remembered that line. He was very delicate.

○

I kept waking up with that panting feeling, waking up really gasping for breath. It was an awful way to wake up, so undignified. It was so stupid that my body thought it should be anxious. Anxiety was a state of excitement, or there was the potential for excitement within it: anxiety was uncertainty. I wasn't uncertain at all, I knew exactly what was coming. The fact that my body thought there was some reason to be hopeful made me even more depressed. When would it realise?

Every night I had some dream of Luke. Sometimes he wasn't in the dream at all, I would be getting ready to go and meet him, standing in front of my mirror actually shaking with excitement. Those preparation dreams were worse than any dreams of Luke himself, they were always full of joy. Some of the dreams with Luke in them were so depressing that they didn't really touch me. I dreamt about an awful holiday we went on to Berlin. The dream was almost a movie, it was full of endless aesthetically coherent scenes. Me and Luke were on the train and my head was lying on his shoulder like a dead thing as he gazed out of the window at a terrible industrial landscape. Then I was lying in a tiny thin-walled room, hearing him have sex with a woman who was wearing a kind of Russian-style fur headpiece and had endlessly long dark hair. There was a scene where I was looking out the window of a train – in my mind Berlin was full of trains – and I was crying, and the scene was almost in black and white, the colours were so weak. It was interesting that my mind could take my feelings and just transpose them to Berlin. I didn't understand the point of that geographical switch.

○

I started having very cold showers. I would get into the shower and feel the water getting colder as I stood in it, I would see my extremities whiten slightly and by the end I would be a weird cold yellow all over. It was distracting to stand in those cold showers in a flood of freezing water. But really the showers did nothing. I felt that I had run out of experiences: I could exercise madly or hurt my body in inconsequential ways or have horrible sex or get drunk. I wasn't sure what else there was to do, there were drugs for sure but it felt very pointless to me, the idea of still living in my mind as it became slightly more random and stupid from drugs. Really I wasn't interested in drugs at all. There was nothing else to do, I had lived every plausible experience, I had carried out each plausible action.

○

Luke sent me a message, the message said Hellooo how are your holidays going?? Then there was a gif of a pink-haired girl in headphones, smiling to herself as she stared at the screen of her computer. Was that girl me, opening Luke's message and reading it, or was it Luke, writing his message to me from his computer in his bedroom? I really didn't know. But some new almost acceptable door opened up to me in that moment, some conceivable future in which me and Luke lived in completely different experiential landscapes but still spoke to one another. Whenever there was some catastrophe we would stop speaking for a week or two and then resume things without acknowledging the crisis, we would simply move away from it silently and passively. We would let that disaster just drift into the past which stretched out behind us almost invisibly, like the wake left by a boat through a river in the dark.

I wrote back in some acceptable way and we made a plan for me to visit Luke in his hometown. Even in this new reality it was possible to make things happen, there were still choices I could make and experiences I could construct for myself. I was different at dinner that night, I spoke and complimented the dinner and everyone was very surprised by that and very grateful.

○

It was hard to get to Luke's hometown from mine, there wasn't really any clear route and I ended up buying lots of different train tickets for different legs of the same very long journey. I left the house when it was actually dark, six twenty in the morning. I had already had an elaborate shower, somehow whenever I saw Luke I wanted to be endlessly clean. It wasn't about my appearance or my physical presentation at all, it was deeper than that. It was very important to be clean. I had a lot of rashes on my body, weird purple rashes like old people's burst veins, but the skin on my face looked very clear, it was unblemished, it was untouched.

The first train of the journey was entirely empty and I listened to an episode of the *New Yorker* fiction podcast out loud from my phone, in which a man's wife inexplicably left him after a terrible tsunami in Japan. When the episode finished I just switched it on again and then on the second and more crowded train I listened to it through headphones. I hadn't heard the story at all somehow so it was good to put it on a second and a third time and I still just heard weird snatches, I heard He no longer had to worry about death or venereal disease, I heard You have nothing inside you that you can give me, I heard Wouldn't the skin itself be the something inside. I didn't feel good at all after listening to that story, I felt very breathless and stayed inside the toilet for a long time with all my things just left behind, lying there on my train seat. Somehow when I got back nobody had stolen those things and I had actually known that nobody would steal them. Things like that never happened to me, things like the theft of all my material possessions.

As the final train was pulling into the station and I was watching the train platform slowing down beside me and stretching out into the body of the station and the whole outside world of Luke's city I did feel a sharp kick of excitement, a sharp kick of almost joy. For a second I felt as if I was inside one of my dreams in which I was about to go meet Luke, deep within a kind of ecstasy. I let myself feel that, I let that feeling survive and almost ran off the train and out of the station. There was Luke, standing in a raincoat and a red hat I had never seen him wear before. I ran for real then, I ran to him and he stood still but held his arms out to show me the place into which I could run: that place right there, the place between his arms. Suddenly the passage of time and the events that had transpired between us didn't matter at all, they barely existed and I was in some totally separate space which was hugging Luke and then walking beside him, gazing up at his face and at the warm and golden hair which fell around it from beneath his hat. Luke had a slight beard suddenly, I said Oh I love your beard and he said You're the first person to see it except my parents, hey you look great. My eyes filled up with tears then but he didn't notice, we just looked up into the trees in the white sunlight.

We walked to a hill, another hill with an outstretched view of the city. We were talking about things that weren't about us, I think we were talking about a group of teenagers in cat ears that Luke had seen on the way to the station, a lot of teenage boys in cat ears. For a second at the top of that hill there and talking about all those catboys I lost comprehension of who I was and what I was seeing and I saw the view as if I was a stranger, just some person seeing some view. I saw generic things, the silhouette of the cathedral, I saw things which were in no sense for or about me, things which would interest many people to a small and forgettable degree. Then I blinked and was myself again. I was overwhelmed by how much was lying there visible to me, by how many things there were, how many meaningful things, an unending number of meaningful things lying down there beneath us.

Luke put on a song from his phone, he put on This Must Be the Place by Talking Heads and said You know this is my favourite song. I had never known that, I had never known Luke's favourite song. Probably it was a song I had heard before without even noticing it, heard in the background of some cafe or on a CD my parents might have played. We sat there on the hill listening to David Byrne softly and gently singing about how it is better not to talk too much about it, how he loves the way time passes and how there was a time before we had been born, how you will love me till the day that my heart stops and I am dead. It was strange to me, how gentle he sounded as he sang these things. The gentleness of his voice almost made me forget that the song was perfect, it was about exactly what I was feeling as I sat there on the hill with Luke beside me and with the past suddenly no longer important or real, with a whole day and night of Luke's company awaiting me there in the future of my life.

We walked, then, to a ruined castle by the river. There were so many families there, so many toddlers falling over one another on the riverbank's soft grass. Me and Luke laughed breathlessly and not at all unkindly at those toddlers as they fell and recovered themselves, and Luke told me an unmemorable anecdote or fact about the history of the castle. We lay on our backs then by the river, and I saw that my T-shirt had ridden up and left my stomach and the bottom of my ribcage exposed. For the first time I really did feel that it was warmer, I felt through the skin of my stomach that the seasons had changed.

It was important, I knew, to focus on the senses without enabling thought. That was at the heart of this day, I thought, as I lay there on the ground beside Luke, as I lay there beside him with his stomach also slightly bare, his shirt also pulled up around his ribcage and a subtle line of fine almost strawberry blonde hair revealed along the centre of his body, leading down into the belted waistband of his shorts. It was important to notice these things without thinking about them, to notice things passively like some dumb creature. Luke pulled a tube of sun cream out of his bag and started covering every visible piece of skin with it, smearing it very precisely into the gaps behind his ears, the exposed section of his neck where his hair ended and his shirt hadn't yet started. He offered me some sun cream, he squeezed it into my wide-open hands and I washed my outstretched arms in it, I washed my neck and face. And so we were protected, our bodies were coated in a white scentless layer which would dissolve if we dove into the river, it would dissolve for sure.

I said Luke would you want to go swimming and he laughed at that: swimming was the kind of whimsical activity that was somehow so ridiculous to imagine doing together but also an activity we were both undeniably drawn to. We were both fascinated by those idyllic kinds of days that we could so easily laugh at and reject. As he was laughing Luke said I mean we actually could, and we walked along the river to a deserted section of river that lay beneath great drooping willow trees, trees which completely lacked density and even materiality, they really had no body and didn't disrupt the falling of the sunlight onto the grass and the water at all.

Suddenly then it was unclear what to do, Luke said I mean were you serious about the swimming thing and I said Only if you want to. We stood there for a minute with that suddenly familiar look passing between us, that suddenly familiar searching look with our eyes locked to each other's eyes and in one rapid movement Luke pulled his shorts down and almost flung his shirt off without even undoing the buttons, it was a very beautiful silky shirt with not many buttons anyway so I could see that that was easy and natural to do and he was standing there then in only his black boxer shorts. Everything was visible to me, each tiny piece of his body and the whole they produced, it was very hard to know where to look or whether to allow myself to just receive some general impression of his body beside me on the riverbank and in a second he was in the water with his body shifting vaguely and greenly beneath the surface.

As I was seeing these things I had been mindlessly removing my own trainers and T-shirt and trousers, weirdly thick and heavy corduroy trousers which I bundled up and left beside Luke's set of things which had come from his body. Luke was so wrong, I was endlessly interested in things. I jumped into the water then, I barely felt it on my skin, it was like my body was just a natural piece of the water and Luke and I were beside each other and completely soaking wet, our hair was dripping streams of water down into our faces and we were grinning across at each other through those little streams of water. I thought of Frank O'Hara, of the tree breathing back and forth between its spectacles. I did understand that sentence now, that wet and endlessly reflected breath.

Luke actually swam then, I was always forgetting that he was athletic and genuinely interested in things like swimming. I treaded water and watched different sections of his body rising and falling from the river, his arms, his legs, his head, I watched the water present these things to me as Luke genuinely swam across the river and then returned and treaded water beside me, the two of us just treading water for a long time as endless things passed beside us, endless feathers, endless leaves and pieces of crisp packet, things which really weren't disgusting to me at all, I would have reached out to touch any one of those things very happily. We were laughing, I think, about some story I was telling about primary school, I was a very bad swimmer and really frightened this girl by using her head as a sort of float and accidentally pushing it under the water and holding it there for more than a minute. The way I told this story it was somehow funny.

After we climbed out of the river we lay there on the ground for a long time, we lay down on nothing and there was mud streaked up our legs because it hadn't been easy to leave the river, we had had to step in mud, to almost claw at it. We lay there with our legs stretched out ahead of us and with tiny trails of mud running between the freckles on our legs. I was very aware and very conscious of some peak within Luke's boxer shorts that I could vaguely see through my peripheral vision, some obscure and possibly imagined peak and I had the accidental sudden thought that it would be so frighteningly easy for me to be crouching beneath him on the riverbank, for my body to be rising and falling with the satisfaction of a great eternal hunger and for Luke to be exhaling as I fed the hunger which lived inside him too, the two of us releasing something there beside the river, releasing the whole stored-up well of energy and tears, even just breath; releasing those things into each other and the air which drifted above us and the riverbank. It was really frightening to me, how easy that would be, how few movements it would require for us to organise our bodies into those positions and to open them up.

I turned those thoughts off then and looked away from Luke into the sky cut through with the vague weak branches of the willow tree. The sky looked and was endless, it was exactly how it looked, endless and stretching out endlessly and so bright blue like some generic perfect sky, distorted and fragmented by nothing. Somehow I did rest, lying beside Luke on the riverbank wearing only an old cotton training bra and some knickers with little glowing oranges patterned into them. We lay there for a long time with the sun falling straight onto our faces and bodies, feeling our faces and bodies being warmed by the sun as we lay beside each other on the ground.

○

Some pattern was making itself visible now, some pattern in which me and Luke lay down beside each other on flat things – some mattresses, some ground – and then, once we got up from those things, we were suddenly flung into an alien type of distance from each other, a contrived kind of distance which Luke was clearly going to great lengths to manufacture and maintain. It was important to him, to destroy that potential, the potential for us to lie down beside each other. We walked along the river in our clothes again and Luke initiated a game where we rated how much we wanted to live in all the houses we passed. There were obviously so many houses I wanted to live in, so many windows revealing scenes I thought looked so appealing, a little desk with a plant on it, an unmade bed, every thing in every window held some dumb appeal for me. Luke's role in his game was problematising all my suggestions, pointing out the subtle but inoperable flaws in every house. He said one perfect house looking out over the river would make us so anxious, seeing dark water moving slowly underneath us from our windows, knowing there was nothing in between our front door and the river. But my anxiety had nothing to do with water or rivers, and Luke knew that. I wondered how many cycles we would pass through in this day and the night which would come after it, how many cycles of contracting and relaxing, of really coming close to something, approximating some truth and then receding from it, watching it recede into nothing.

○

Luke showed me his favourite tree, it was a quite normal-looking birch tree on the corner of a street. Would

I ever in the whole course of my life meet another man who had a favourite tree, a favourite tree which was really just some random tree on a street corner. We stood there for a long time looking at the tree and my mood really changed as we stood there, I suddenly felt that Luke did want to give me a part of him, he wanted me to take his favourite tree and place it inside of my memory.

We walked along an endless stretch of highway to Luke's house, we stood for a long time waiting to cross at the roundabout as endless drivers passed us, saw us standing there together by the highway. It didn't feel very convincing to me, to be standing with Luke beside a highway, it was hard to contextualise him inside any kind of mental understanding of motor traffic. After that highway we passed a long stretch of road through some slight forest, an abandoned service station by the roadside. I told Luke I thought we could climb onto the roof of that service station and he agreed, probably we would be able to do that, but what would be the point. He was right, there really would be no point in doing it.

○

It was three o'clock then and we hadn't eaten, this seemed like a big deal to Luke and I was happy to defer to the alleged importance of distinctions between hours in the day. We rushed to his house, we almost ran up so many streets and up a hill. When we arrived there was a Greek salad in the fridge which he had prepared earlier, that was such an unreal, intoxicating image, Luke standing in his parents' kitchen cutting up cucumbers and tomatoes and tossing them with salad leaves and crumbling some feta into the bowl to prepare something for us to eat together. We would eat that meal beside one another in his very light kitchen filled with windows, really all the walls of that kitchen were windows, every wall. There were peaches and cold beers in the fridge and Luke handed me those too so that I was standing there holding those beers and firm cold peaches and somehow also our bowl of salad, and Luke was laughing and taking the things out of my hands again. Luke just stood there taking those things out of my hands and placing them onto the table with his own hands, his hands which had touched so many things that day, the sun cream, the river, his hands which held so many experiences.

I was thinking, as Luke took those things from me, about whether each specific moment was defined by the things which were to come and the things which had already taken place, or whether each moment could take on a kind of independent existence and define itself, and live forever in a reality totally untouched by the past and by the future. I almost felt that there might be a way to take my perception in that moment and to freeze it as some self-sustaining thing, unaffected by whatever was still going to happen between me and Luke and whatever impenetrable things had already happened. Really all I wanted was Luke inside his kitchen surrounded by things to eat and drink and with the sun flung over everything so that everything was warm and clearly visible, each one of his freckles illuminated. That was all I ever wanted.

○

We went into the garden where Luke's parents were sitting on garden furniture. Luke's father was a thin intellectual-seeming man and briefly thought I was some girl called Evie. It turned out that Evie was a friend Luke had in school, it seemed like a really long time ago, it seemed like even primary school. Luke explained that I wasn't Evie without saying my actual name. No this isn't Evie, he said. His parents wanted my opinion on a problem related to his sister's wedding. The wedding was going to be in their garden that summer. Luke's parents were worried that the children who came might fall into the pond which lay behind us in the grass. It seemed like this was a problem they discussed a lot as a family and I found it hard to feel involved, I found it hard to feel worried about children falling into the pond. How deep could this pond be, why couldn't the children climb out of it, it wasn't clear to me at all. I hadn't known that Luke's sister was going to be married.

Suddenly then everyone became aware of a much more urgent problem, everyone realised this problem at once and started talking about it very rapidly and impenetrably. Eventually I understood that Luke's parents had left a mattress for me to sleep on in the garage but because I was a girl this was no longer acceptable, the mattress would have to be moved. When they left to go and move the mattress I didn't want Luke to even mention that conversation to me, I didn't want to talk about it. It was very depressing to me, that Luke's parents had expected me to be a boy. Somehow that revealed some awful fundamental things in how Luke thought of me, I didn't want to even think about Luke's parents dragging a mattress across the dusty concrete floor of the garage because I wasn't a boy.

○

Luke and I went for a drink that night, for no reason we invented a false version of our situation in which I was really underdressed and so Luke lent me his coat, a heavy sort of blue-grey raincoat with a thick artificial wool lining. It was quite a strange coat and very engulfing as we walked along the street, I did that coat up as far as I could and was encompassed in its heavy skin. A fox hissed at us as we walked along the pavements, an invisible fox but Luke was sure it was a fox, he felt that there was nothing else it could be, nothing else could hiss like that.

Luke bought me a drink once we arrived, a delicious glass of pale yellow beer, and bought himself two pints of beer at once, two pints which came together in a really insane bucket-sized glass. That was very funny to us, Luke drinking his beer from this extremely large glass and I was suddenly happy in that moment. It always delighted me when Luke bought me things, it made me feel like he really did want me there beside him, he wanted me there badly enough to buy me things which would tie me even tighter to that place in which I was, the place beside him. And he wasn't scared to drink with me, which meant he wasn't scared I'd cross some line and hurt him. We sat outside the pub, there was a very warm glowing atmosphere even though I don't remember seeing any lights there; we sat opposite each other in the inexplicably warm light.

We were talking about books that night. Luke told me his favourite book was about a very old man depressingly ageing and losing his mind and I said I really admire how your favourite book actually has nothing to do with you. All of my favourite books were about vaguely disembodied cerebral girls and if I wrote some book it would be about a vaguely disembodied cerebral girl too, I told Luke this but suddenly I couldn't think of any examples. Maybe I had made that idea up, the idea of all those countless favourite books about those disembodied girls. I couldn't think of a single one of those girls, in that moment.

We talked, then, about creative pursuits, how we both had this deeply rooted feeling that we had the potential to really succeed at some creative pursuit even though this was obviously an extremely arrogant idea. Luke said I don't even know what I see myself doing, if it's music or writing or even visual art. That concept was so funny to us then or maybe it was more the phrase Visual Art that was funny, I said I never really love visual art except if I like the meaning but then I would rather have a book or song about that meaning. Luke agreed, he said We are not hedonistic enough to enjoy paintings. He really was right about that, neither of us was driven by hedonism at all. Things might have turned out differently if me and Luke were more hedonistic, more engaged with the aesthetics of visual art.

○

Somehow Luke didn't want us to be inside his house yet, we went for a long walk through streets. As we walked past the front gardens of suburban houses almost invisible in the night we were talking about the thoughts men might have about me. Luke said that men would think I was like some film character, that even when I was angry or awkward I was angry or awkward in the way that film characters were, not in a grating real-life way but like some fake invented person. I don't know what kind of person would be able to engage with that, he said. I said What do you mean and he said I just find it really hard to imagine the type of person you would date. It would have to be such a specific person, he said. I said Specific like how and he said No I really don't know, that's what I'm saying, I can't picture that person.

I had no answer to that question, to the eternal question of what kind of man would ever be able to speak to me. I kicked a stone into the road and accidentally hit a car with the stone and dented its body in a subtle but irreparable way. Luke didn't notice, he was too busy looking away from me, looking at some walls in front of houses so he didn't have to see that I was for some reason crying in the middle of the street and in the dark. But when I made some dreadful wet inhalation sound he looked at me, he turned to me and said Hey I'm sorry, I can feel I'm talking about things in a careless way. I really am sorry about everything, he said, in the same alien tone he'd used as I had lain there on his mattress in the dark.

Right at that moment he embraced me and even as he was embracing me I didn't understand what it was that I was feeling, what the feeling of his arms so warm and heavy on my shoulders was. I couldn't understand what my wet face was pressed against, what steady form stroked the hair which had tucked itself inside the neck of Luke's old raincoat, its ends hidden. In that moment I didn't understand what material reality was causing those sensations, but still in some other part of my brain I breathed Luke into me, I breathed in his smell which I was always so reluctant to describe even inside of my own mind because I knew that I couldn't explain it at all. It wasn't made up of other already known smells but was distinct and therefore totally inexpressible. Forever I would be alone with my own knowledge of Luke's smell, clean and good and yet specific to the body that was his alone, and that could never be faked by using chemicals or toiletries or some specific washing powder. Once he was gone all of those senses would be gone from me.

As we walked from that embrace towards Luke's house I wondered if that moment could have been some version of the love that I had wanted: Luke having pushed me far enough away from him to hold me tenderly there; Luke really holding me there as I cried and cried in the dark streets of his childhood. I kept wondering that until we were back inside his house.

○

After all this I now had to lie down and sleep in the spare room of Luke's family home, on top of the mattress which had been placed in the centre of the room by his two parents. This seemed very cruel, almost unbearably cruel, like some parody of an abject, humiliating situation: sleeping alone in this random room in Luke's childhood home as he slept in his own double bed in some place unreachably far above me. It felt too extreme to be devastating, like something that might happen in a very metaphorical story I might write, that image of Luke asleep in his bed and me lying there on some old mattress very far beneath him.

The spare room was full of miscellaneous things: a toy microscope, some steel toolboxes, the board game Mouse Trap, a knitted quilt in baby colours. It was unclear what kind of person this room was used by, what kind of room it was at all as I stood there in the doorway with Luke about to absent himself and leave me to lie down alone inside the room in which so many different things from his family's past had come to die.

Luke's childhood rabbit was in there too, nuzzling around. I didn't understand why this rabbit was still alive, I suddenly remembered a story Luke had told me on the phone about the rabbit: he'd been given it for his ninth birthday and had used it to practice football with, kicking a ball for the rabbit to chase and somehow return to him. When I asked him about this he said the rabbit was very old, and it did, suddenly, seem old, slow, almost dead, mindlessly shoving its face into whatever soft objects it encountered. It was just pushing things around endlessly there, pushing at Luke's old childhood games and blankets stupidly and eternally.

Luke was ready for bed, then. He told me where in the house his room was even though I already knew, I had been inside his room and seen him lying there on his childhood bed beneath the old Egyptian organ pot. I guess he had forgotten that. Luke said that he was telling me these things in case I needed him in the night, that was the phrase he used, In case you need me. That sentence, too, felt painfully cruel. We both knew that there were no situations left in which I would be able to come to the door of Luke's room and stand outside of it saying I need you. All of those situations had been used up already.

○

For probably five hours I lay there awake on the ground. Every few minutes I would start with a jolt as if I was falling or dropping something fundamental and had to urgently lunge forward to catch it, I couldn't even tell if I was really moving my body or if I was imagining the movement in my stupid half-sleep. Eventually I did fall asleep after I had taken my clothes off and was lying there naked with the curtains open and vague light from the streetlamps falling between Luke's old objects. In my half-sleep I had the idea that it would be some very positive thing, if Luke or even his parents walked in on me lying there naked in the morning. Somehow I thought that that would bring about some great positive change, I really thought that it might bring me something valuable, something indispensable.

○

Luke and I ate breakfast together in the garden in our pyjamas. We talked about porridge and cereal, how they were similar and how they were different and what were the advantages and disadvantages of each. Luke said I always pictured you being a two-breakfast-item girl, but I wasn't, I was a one-breakfast-item girl, I ate a bowl of his Bran Flakes and a coffee he had made. It was an instant coffee. Life really betrayed me, in some small but heavy way, through the insertion of that instant coffee into the morning. In every mental image I had of me and Luke spending a morning together we were drinking real coffee which one of us had made on the stovetop or inside a cafetière, that was one of the least disposable images, one of the most essential ones.

That morning Luke was operating under the assumption that I had to make a very specific train and that this train was in the late morning just before lunch. We walked around a pet fish shop before I went to the station. In some other mood that shop might have been aesthetic to me and even a joyful and hilarious thing for me and Luke to do together, but on this morning just before I had to leave to go and make some arbitrary train it was depressing. It felt like the deletion of a morning, wandering around, looking at fish. I took some photos of Luke standing among fish tanks in the dark but that didn't help, it was still depressing to be with Luke surrounded by fish in bright blue tanks and talking about the fish and what their types were, what the types looked like and what they did, which was the same for all the types, it was to swim around the fish tanks.

Luke walked me to the station then. I wondered if it was because I was a girl or maybe because of the movies I had seen that train stations felt like the sites of great romantic potential to me. Luke was clearly not feeling the situational pressure of the train station at all even as we stood outside the entrance facing one another and about to say goodbye. I made a random unfunny joke where I pretended to push my whole hand inside his mouth, I dragged this joke out for a long time until we hugged goodbye in one brief sudden moment across so many impermeable layers of jackets and bags. That was it, Luke walked away from me. I knew from the direction he was walking that he was walking to the river and that was endlessly poignant to me, that image of Luke walking away from me in the direction of the river, Luke about to walk along the river in some direction which was away from me. Probably never again would I see him walking away from me in the direction of a river. I tried to pull some plausible situation out of my mind in which I could stop him from leaving and call him back to me, some situation where I wouldn't end up getting on that randomly chosen train and going to some place very far away from him. I stood there for a long time thinking about that.

○

The train Luke had chosen for me was not efficient, I had to change trains in London and the second train I had a ticket for was cancelled so I went to sit in a park somewhere and waited for the next one. I sat on the grass and felt the whole ground shaking as the Tube passed underneath it, I felt the ground vibrating as if we were in the middle of some natural disaster movie and no one even looked up, no one thought that it was strange. All around me people were moving as if they didn't know it was impossible to transport oneself in any meaningful way and I just had to sit there on the ground and feel them move. I had to sit there on the ground above the trains and fully surrounded by things which only spoke of Luke to me, the grass, the sky, even my trousers and my shoes, all of these things which meant nothing to me except for him. I didn't know how to reconcile those two thoughts:

that it was impossible to transport oneself out of anywhere and that I was surrounded by things which shouted out Luke's name eternally.

○

The rest of the holiday went quickly. I just studied a lot. I studied questions of memory and vision, questions of language and representation and transaction and thought. These things that I was learning were the last things that would ever be given to me. Anything else that I wanted to know I would have to seek out for myself. The knowledge wouldn't be spontaneous, it would be some already existent part of me multiplying itself outwards. It was very strange, that this was what I was left with: a complicated drawing of the human eye, a timeline of a baby's language learning, a theory someone had made up about symbols and meaning. These things were the last fragments of something that had once been mine. Sometimes I would think about that and then wonder if I should do a Master's but that was never what I meant at all, I was always annoyed with myself for simplifying my thoughts into some neat actionable conclusion. Any plausible solution was very far beside the point, and very trite.

○

I got a manicure for some reason, I paid over thirty pounds for a manicure. I sat inside a salon as a woman scraped away at the fabric of my nails with a fine and rapidly moving drill skidding all over my nails and grating them down. It was amazing, how much surplus trust I was expected to contain, how much trust I was assumed to have just lying there inside of me and ready to offer to a stranger scraping away at the living surface of my nails. I told myself it couldn't hurt but it did hurt me. My nails looked very shallow at the end. They did look like a woman's nails but they also looked very sunken.

○

Two days later I went back to university. That journey was strange, the whole way there I felt uneasy and creeped out even. I knew it was the last time I would be in a car going back to university but it felt endlessly repetitive to me, that journey to and from university. I felt that the journey represented something, something about the incessant nature of my life. I could be in a car driving to or from university and be feeling anything, and regardless of how I was feeling I would be stuck inside that car knowing that I would be on that same exact journey at some point in the future, feeling some other way and with some other endless set of things having happened to me and some other endless set of things awaiting me.

There was no way to change the fact that time would pass and things would happen, things like lying alone on the floor of Luke's spare room, seeing the sea crashing depressingly against some pier, seeing Nick's penis flapping around between my legs, endless things like that.

That night I had a nightmare. Luke was driving, I was in the back, and I didn't know where he was taking me. I ooked down at my body then and saw that it was totally smooth all over like an elbow or a heel, I had no genitals at all, just pale yellow skin covering the place between my legs. In the dream I knew, then, where Luke was taking me, I knew and I felt some great shot of dread and recognition too: I knew that terrible place very well. But when I woke up I couldn't remember where that place was.

○

Luke didn't write to me for several days, even once term started he didn't write to me and he didn't answer when I knocked on his door, he wasn't behind his door, his food wasn't in the fridge. It made me nauseous, looking at his empty white shelf of fridge. I felt that I could write some novel like *The Bell Jar* but instead of opening with a passage about the death penalty it would open with Luke's empty white fridge shelf. That empty shelf was just as frightening, just as full of sick foreboding.

I started sending him an increasingly random set of

messages, I really didn't know what sort of message would make him respond to me so I just kept sending different messages in different tones and genres. He didn't respond to any of them, he didn't even read them, they just stayed delivered, they had been delivered to his phone. I really didn't know what sort of message Luke might want to receive from me.

I didn't really study, then. I spent a lot of time just lying around outside like a dead fish. I felt weirdly relaxed, I felt depressed for sure but also quite relaxed, it was easy for me to spend hours just lying around in the park with my eyes shut. Then after a couple of days I became nauseous and developed a temperature and threw up into the bath. According to the internet I had heat stroke, based on my temperature and the vomiting the internet said I should call 999 and I almost laughed at that. This was no emergency, that was clear to me. I was fine, I recovered by myself after I lay in my bed for a long time with wet rags flung over my body and my eyes pressed very tightly shut.

○

One night that week I activated the fire extinguisher in the corridor between Luke's room and mine, I broke the seal on that fire extinguisher and its creamy white foam started releasing itself everywhere, all over the wooden walls and the carpet and the heavy door of the kitchen.

I didn't know how to respond to the situation I had created and just left the fire extinguisher there in the hallway as it kept streaming more and more foam onto the floor. I could hear it from my room, sighing out its heavy white substance. It didn't sound urgent, the exhalation of that fire extinguisher, it sounded casual and passive, a quiet endless seeping.

The next morning the whole block got an email about the fire extinguisher, they wanted to know who had done it, who had set it off. Luke, too, would have received that email, Luke too would have found out that a person had set off the fire extinguisher in the corridor outside of his room. I worried then that that was why I'd done it, so that Luke would receive an email about it and know it had been me, that I had caused that endless seeping. It was hard to know how much I knew, how much Luke knew and how much both of us were blind to. Someone had already cleaned up the foam and I did feel bad about that, there was no reason why anyone should have to do extra cleaning because of my own private demonstrations of distress. I hadn't thought about that part of setting off the fire extinguisher, the part where the foam would have to get cleaned up.

○

The next day Luke did text me, he said that he was going to complete the final section of his Master's from his parents' house. This text was so frightening that I read it without moving my eyes, I read it in a single moment and the moment had no duration at all, it was an unsplittable moment. Somehow I was immediately convinced that Luke was leaving because of me, that he felt that I was causing him some great and unbearable harm. He had to get out, I was eating away at him slowly and I might really hurt him if he stayed. He didn't know what I might do to him, what kind of harm I might cause in the future.

After some time this idea was no longer vivid or palpable to me, I wasn't sure that Luke felt like I was hurting him, I wasn't sure he felt like I was able to touch him at all. I was left with nothing then, I was left with the knowledge that Luke was leaving me for some reason I couldn't understand or even guess at. I knew nothing about Luke, his feelings were completely obscure to me and would remain obscure forever as he sat there alone at his parents' kitchen table and I sat alone at the desk inside my wooden room with some small amount of light seeping in through the dirty slanted windows. We would never know each other, we would never reach each other, we were like the matching poles of magnets repelling each other, with one of the magnets desperately moving towards the other but being unable to resist that great force of repulsion generated out of nowhere, and existing simply because of the immovable laws of nature.

That afternoon I realised that I had been missing the

point of Luke's text entirely. The central fact of the situation was suddenly very obviously that Luke and I might never again be in the same physical space. There was no longer any kind of external reality which tied us together. All that tied me to Luke now was my love for him, my love which he so desperately wanted to kill. I went for a run right then in my normal clothes and ran into a lamppost on purpose, my face and chest and stomach all colliding with the metal pole at once, in one great shock, and for one moment I was saved by that stunning oblivion.

○

I spent a long time that afternoon throwing hair ties into the road and watching what happened to them, watching them be run over by cars. The presence of those hair ties didn't affect the cars at all, they were so small that the tyres couldn't even touch them, they were completely undetectable.

I went back to my room then and took a million photos of the things in my and Luke's kitchen: the toaster, the fridge, the stovetop, the oily window. I was crying as I took those photos, some boy came into the kitchen and I said Fuck off while looking right into his eyes. He left immediately, then. It frightened me, that I had told the boy to fuck off, that I had told him to fuck off in a way that made him actually leave. Why had I said that?

When I got back to my room I saw that my trousers were completely soaked through and heavy with blood. In that moment it wasn't even clear to me that the blood was my period, it felt like the blood might be coming from a source much deeper inside me, wet red blood flowing right out of my heart. I just threw those dripping things into the bin then. In the shower the water stayed red the whole time, the water never ran clear, I was still half covered in blood when I got out of the shower. I couldn't be bothered to keep standing there until I was clean. I couldn't wait for that indeterminate amount of time, I really couldn't.

○

I started having some new experience, I would remember just totally involuntarily some moment Luke and I had spent together, some random inconsequential thing that he had said to me and I would be immediately sobbing then, sobbing in an awful gasping way, I would be clinging on to the things around me in order to steady myself like a tragic sort of soap opera character. It felt biological, that sobbing, it felt like a reflex, like the reflex reaction that a leg would have to being hit on the exact right section of the knee. I was a body collapsing onto the bed with an unstoppable well of tears falling out from behind my eyes. It wasn't an emotional process, it was an arrow running straight from memory to bodily response.

Yet the things I was remembering were not important. I was remembering how Luke had one time talked to me through the phone about how easy it was to lie on the phone, you couldn't see that other person's face or body and so you could easily just lie to them almost accidentally. I had agreed with him, I had said I also found it so easy to lie by accident through the phone. Had I really felt that way? I couldn't remember. I was remembering a time when I had been making this awful lentil spaghetti and had offered it to Luke to try and placed my fork inside his mouth and he'd agreed, those lentil noodles were disgusting. I was remembering the dry sandy texture of those noodles, their real tastelessness.

There were weeks and weeks of memories like that which I had forgotten and which were now pouring back into me like some Biblical flood or plague, the plague of locusts, the plague of darkness, the plague of water turning into blood. It was impossible to forget these things. It wasn't that the memories acquired some new meaning as I looked back on them as static dead things from the past. The specific features of those memories weren't important at all, they really had no meaning. The memories were all significant for the same reason, which was that they included Luke, Luke speaking to me intentionally through the phone or from some real place beside me, Luke speaking words which he was creating specifically and purposefully and only for me, for me alone to hear.

I was granted permission to type my finals, some authority had decided that my handwriting was sufficiently bad for that exemption to be made since I was dyspraxic. I was always forgetting that I had a disorder of movement, some real disorder in the way that I related to the world. This exemption was obviously positive, I did badly when I had to handwrite my essays, no one could read them and the effort it took to write legibly made it impossible for me to really think. Still it depressed me, to receive this exemption. There was so much that had to be done to me before I was legible, so many mediating layers of other people's inventions. It made me think of all those shoes and doorways stuck inside of Luke's computer. How were they doing now, how far along was Luke with his project? Maybe they had been created already, maybe they were just sitting there inside his computer waiting for the time when he would graduate and they could finally be deleted. They were just waiting for that moment when they could go away and would no longer have to sit there in the mind of his computer at all.

Luke wrote back to me, this reminded me that I had written to him, I hadn't felt like I was waiting for a response from him at all. He said that he was feeling overwhelmed and wanted to prioritise his Master's, that was why he wasn't coming back to university. This text was worse than the blank absence of a text. Luke was saying nothing, all he was doing was drawing attention to the things he was leaving unsaid. What was overwhelming Luke, what was his Master's taking priority over? Those verbs made no sense without the existence of some external body which was oppressing him and which he was choosing to let die in service of his Master's degree. He was using language wrong, he was speaking in some very partial way which ignored relationality and consequence, as if he could have feelings and desires which were produced from an entirely insulated place inside himself.

I wondered if it was even real, Luke's preoccupation with his Master's. It assumed a high level of optimism, some intense amount of interest in the future and in jobs, even, to care so much about degree results. I sent him a very stupid reply about how climate change was coming and he shouldn't waste time, he should focus on the present and not live in service of the future. I wasn't sure if the message was meant to be a joke or not. I felt guilty then, things like climate change really did make Luke anxious. Luke's anxiety had a very broad perspective on the world.

Luke didn't reply to the thing about climate change, I really wished I hadn't sent it. I couldn't understand why

I was being so bad towards him, I couldn't understand it at all. All I wanted was to be lying next to him and fully listening to him and to the reasons why he was feeling overwhelmed and wanted to study his Master's from home. That was really all I wanted, to be running my fingers through his hair as he talked and talked about the things that he was feeling. What I wanted was something precise and something plausible, too, it wasn't at all far from the things we'd done together in the winter, in the autumn. I did just miss Luke, it didn't have to be some complicated thing, I did just miss him and want to be beside him. It wasn't even strange or bad that I wanted that, no one would think that it was strange if it wasn't for the fact that Luke wanted to be so far away from me.

I felt, then, that some very bad and twisted thing had been created for no reason at all, something dark and almost sinister had been born out of the fact that I just loved Luke and wanted to be next to him and listening to him and looking up at him. All I wanted was me and Luke lying awake in the morning feeling the sun rising over our bodies, feeling our bodies being drenched in golden sunlight. I'd be lying there knowing that at any moment I could look to the side and see him beside me or behind me there. It was so easy to imagine: the sun falling straight onto our bodies through the windows and blinds, so that our bodies became patterned with the objects that stood in between us and the world.

I had my first exam that week. Because I was typing my exams I had to do them in this dark circular room in the psychology department. Everyone else's exams were in a sports hall and I developed a really idealised vision of that sports hall, in my mind it was in a beautiful dense forest and had lush green floors stretched out ahead of everyone, in front of their desks. Some man was in the private room to supervise me, a PhD student I think, a man with a brown beard. I had an instinctual feeling he was unwashed and quite dirty even though he didn't seem dirty in any material way. I think by that feeling I just meant that I really didn't want him there in that room with me.

The exam question was a trick, it was a very vague general question about how to understand causality rather than a question about any material topic. I knew exactly what type of answer I had to produce, I had to say that it was very difficult to understand causality but that it would eventually be possible if we took every aspect of each conceivable situation into account and eliminated all of those aspects, if we really destroyed those situational details. Then I had to give an endless list of examples of all those things which should be destroyed in all those situations.

I pointlessly invented a false experiment to base my essay around, the experiment was conducted by a man called Heigel in the mid-twentieth century. Heigel's experiment involved some very complicated maze-like mouse traps and random manipulations of different aspects of the mice's situations, for example some were in the light and others were in the dark, some had had their brains destroyed and others had not. From this experiment Heigel discovered that it was possible to predict every movement each mouse made when all of its conditions were known and controlled for, and that causality is real and true. Everything can be understood very easily and completely when enough information is gathered, that was the conclusion of Heigel's experiment and of my essay and I really did mean it, I really did believe that everything operated under some complex unknowable logic, I still believed that back then.

I wasn't at all worried by the fact that I had grounded my essay in this fake study. Really any study could be real, no one could ever be marked down for having written some false thing because in reality anything could be true. This was something a lecturer had actually told us. No one ever had enough information to make that judgement, the judgement that something was false. Through inventing that Heigel study I was just taking those ideas about causality to their natural conclusion: some things were true and some were false, some things would occur and other things would never become real but no person would ever know enough to really give meaning to those distinctions. There was truth but we would never access that truth.

○

I went on another date with Nick, the date was sitting in his room. He had put up some more pictures on his walls, a photocopy of a photograph of a woman lying on the ground underneath leaves. The photograph was obviously meant to be arousing, the woman's naked body engulfed there in wet debris, her eyes closed and her head tilted back so passive and dead. Abject death was very arousing, you were supposed to think, when you looked at the photograph. Then next to it there was a picture of two men looking down a metal tube. The picture was taken from the point of view of someone lying right inside that tube so that all you could see was those men's eyes and then some parts of their noses and cheeks. Those men were just staring down at us through their slightly reflective metal tube.

Nick told me about a film he was going to make after he graduated. The film was going to be about a young man found dead on a hillside, on top of a large flat stone. Through uncovering the reasons for his death, questions about human nature, and more specifically about nationalism, would be addressed. Nick was vague about whether this would be a feature film or a documentary, he really didn't know, the question wasn't even relevant to him somehow. He was talking as if there was some real man lying dead on a hillside somewhere just waiting for Nick to look at him if he decided, in the end, that his film would be a documentary and not a feature film.

Nick showed me a stack of books he had bought to research his film. The books were ancient-looking history books with soft fabric covers and random men's names engraved into their spines. They were about things like World War II aircraft or World War I flu. Did Nick really believe that these books would lead him towards any kind of meaningful knowledge of the world? I could imagine him standing in some secondhand bookshop holding them, I could imagine him carrying them to the till to pay for them, taking his debit card out of his wallet, paying for them with his credit card.

After he had told me about his film Nick said Shall we, he said Shall we just like Guy had said it, in that same uninterested tone of voice with that weirdly ironic and almost unkind edge to it. I had the thought then that I just wanted someone to be desperately hungry for my body, I wanted someone to be unable to resist how much they very badly wanted me but I don't know why that was a thought I had, nothing would have been better if Nick had been desperately hungry for my body, things might even have been worse. We became naked then and Nick gracelessly threw me down onto his bed and started pushing himself onto me, just pushing himself there with my face pressed to his chest so that I didn't have to even kiss him, I just had to lie there very still in a slightly folded shape. I thought about that suicide lecture from the winter as Nick pushed himself against me, about suicide as a solution to the excessively porous boundaries of the self. My self was very discrete, its boundaries were endlessly clear.

I tried very hard, as I lay there, to imagine how some situation like this could ever feel arousing and fulfilling to me, how it could ever feel even acceptable, to be lying there closed or even to open myself as I lay on the top of a mattress with a man pushing himself onto me harshly and pointlessly and with my face just lying stuck beneath his damp and wide chest. Maybe there would be situations like that, maybe in the future this would be something I loved and relished and I would look back on the past with pity and real incomprehension. It really was possible. I got dressed and walked home then, along the side of the road until I was back inside my room and alone. I could fall asleep and when I woke up some other endless set of things would begin happening, another day would start.

○

The whole next day I sat in the library eating different treats I bought from the library cafe, so many small soft cookies. That did help me, the feeling and the taste of those soft cookies in my mouth, and they were cheap, too, and I could buy a bitter and watery coffee. There really were things that I could do to make myself feel better, there were lots of things I could ingest. I sat there eating those things in the deserted library with its thick glass windows which I saw through my own thick glasses. The sky was grey. The windows weren't uplifting in that moment, the light from outside wasn't energising.

I was trying to write a story about this woman stuck inside of her apartment, that was the premise of the story, this woman who couldn't leave her apartment for some reason. But I couldn't describe that situation for more than a couple of pages, something else needed to happen. I added some details about the woman going to bed and waking up again, walking out to the supermarket, smoking cigarettes out of her window, even sending this man Xavier an endless list of texts and all these very distressed voicemails. Still it felt like a terrible story. Things kept happening, the story would reach some emotional peak, the woman would be close to death and then some random other paragraph would follow and completely deflate things, really strip my story of direction and of meaning.

Was I very bad at writing? That just felt like life to me, random things happening on and on. Nothing was ever allowed to be the end, some unbearable thing would happen and then some slightly less awful but still painful things would happen, then some other unbearable thing, then some other slightly bad things, on and on forever. I didn't understand why every novel wasn't just an endless depressing list of pointless things that happened. I gave up on my story then and went back to my room.

○

Lots of time passed, multiple weeks of me just studying in glass libraries and studying in my room and taking exams in that circular room and then sitting in my own room and maybe crying slightly or sending Luke some texts which he would not respond to or eating random foods just quietly there by myself. It was really hot during those weeks, my whole body was lying around at the mercy of the sun and the hot air. I think the sun was actually damaging my hair. My hair was breaking, it was filling up with split ends in places where they made no sense, all over this new layer of hair on the top of my head. There were so many new hairs up there which were coming out already full of split ends, hairs which were born somehow completely destroyed. My body was trying to tell me it was dying, it was destroying all the things which were the easiest to destroy and then it would move on to the more unkillable things. I had that thought a lot then, about all those unkillable things that would die inside my body.

○

In a few days I would turn twenty-one, I texted Luke this and asked if he wanted to meet up on my birthday. My exams would be over then, my exams were over very easily and quickly with a final practical exam which asked me to solve a million questions about probability. What was the probability of different things? Was the probability high? Or was it small, so small that it wasn't really a probability at all but just some randomly generated thing that the world had created by accident? So many different things could happen in the world, almost all of them were accidents and therefore insignificant and those insignificant things should be discounted and forgotten forever, that was the moral of my statistics exam.

Luke texted me back and said that he would come visit me on my birthday, his exams would be over by then also. He would come see me and also David. As soon as I got this text I went for a walk, I walked over the river leading out into the city and the river was lit up with sun, speckled with painfully bright reflected flecks of it. There was a dead rat lying in the middle of the pavement at the end of the bridge. I took a photo of that rat, I was also in the photo, it was a selfie of me standing over that old dead rat. I don't know why I wanted that photo, that selfie of me over the body of some dead grey rat, but somehow I really did want it.

○

I woke up early on the day when Luke was coming and I wasn't sure what to do with myself, I wasn't sure where to put myself or my body until he arrived. I spent a long time putting on a very stupid outfit, it was the outfit that a parody of a tennis player girl might wear, some bright blue sports skirt I had worn as a twelve-year-old and a sort of see-through knitted vest. I could really wear anything at any time, I almost looked quite nice, I looked inexplicably tanned and closer to a cheerleader girl from a movie than I had ever looked before in my life. I went and bought three doughnuts from a Krispy Kreme shop in a shopping centre like a boring greedy child in an American film.

Luke called me once I was back in my room and eating a wet Biscoff-flavoured doughnut, he said he was arriving now and on his way to go meet David who lived extremely far away, close to the hospital. Luke might be a long time, he might be many hours, I think he was saying, I barely heard the words because I'd started to cry and I wasn't sure what type of crying it was, what emotion it stemmed from. Luke said Sorry is it okay if

I get to you by like mid-afternoon and I said Okay okay okay about a million times and he put the phone down then. It was impossible to evaluate whether that had been a normal phone call but Luke didn't text me. Maybe it had been normal or maybe he didn't notice those things anymore. Maybe that was some category of thing he no longer had to engage with: my emotions heard through the phone.

I lay down on the floor and listened to random music from Spotify. I listened to Fiona Apple, Spotify was very insistent that I listen to Fiona Apple in that moment, every section of Spotify was screaming out her name: the Recommended Artists section, the Trending Albums for You section, even some section called You are the main character. I was the main character in my own life and Fiona Apple was the soundtrack, that was the message that Spotify was sending me. For almost two hours I listened to a Fiona Apple song called I Want You to Love Me and I felt as if I had written it myself, the part about how next year it'll be clear, about how all my particles will disband and disperse, about how while I'm in this body I want you to love me, how I've been waiting for you to love me, just waiting on and on for you to love me. It really was true, it was so true that it almost didn't feel real. It felt like an approximation or a huge oversimplification of something, it felt false in that way because it was so abjectly true.

At half past three Luke texted to say that we could meet on the road which led to the hospital, he was ready. I walked there almost passively, almost without feeling, suddenly it barely mattered to me whether Luke and I saw each other or not. Our relationship had nothing to do with situations like seeing one another on the street and talking, our relationship was completely untethered from any plausible acts we could engage in, together or apart. I saw him walking towards me then and I didn't speed up. It felt in that moment like if I started to run he would immediately stand still and we wouldn't end up beside one another any sooner than we would have if we had both walked slowly and placidly along the street. I really did feel that he would do that, that he would stand very still in order to maintain some false and arbitrary sense of equilibrium between us, in service of some private goal which was for me to stay very far away from him.

We reached each other then and Luke said Happy birthday. I said How's David. Luke told me a long story about some problem that was happening between David and Callum involving someone's ex-girlfriend. He told me a second story then about how he had been talking to an intriguing girl on the internet. This girl sent him millions of Snapchats but the Snapchats were things like a dark photo of her bedroom with almost nothing visible, only the faint spooky outline of her desk or the end of her bed. She creeped him out but still she was really compelling to him. He was just worried that she was a robot or even that she was underage, so he didn't send her anything, he just said things like Hi and Hey and waited for the girl to send him another creepy blank photo.

I wondered whether Luke was actively trying to alienate me, as we walked like that along the road, whether he was trying to make me hate his company so that he could leave and go back home. I walked along the street looking at the ground, watching the ground so intently as if I was looking for some kind of movement.

We went into a cafe and Luke bought a decaffeinated coffee. He poured some of the coffee into a glass which was standing on the counter, possibly that glass wasn't even clean, I thought I saw some dirty fingerprints on its insides. The coffee in the glass was for me and Luke's coffee was the coffee in the mug. Once I was finished he refilled the glass with some more coffee from the mug which made the separation between mug and glass pointless: the coffee which had touched Luke's body was entering my body anyway. He bought me a random piece of gluten-free lemon cake. That didn't feel like any kind of gift to me, Luke hadn't given me a birthday present or even a card and I felt that that was a very active step that he was taking away from me. Maybe one of Luke's friends had advised him not to give me a birthday card, maybe David had. Maybe David had said Luke be careful, don't give her anything. Maybe David had said Luke remember, anything you give her she will use against you.

At six Luke went to get his train, he said his journey would be very long, too long to undertake while it was dark. He was talking like someone on an ancient pilgrimage, it was very important to him that it would still be light when he got back to his parents' house. We said goodbye then, and Luke told me he would have a party soon for his own birthday. We would see each other then, at the birthday party. I said Okay and Luke walked into the station and away from me, I couldn't even see him walking through the ticketed gates. The station wasn't busy at all, I don't know why I couldn't see the gates. I wondered in a vague way whether that would count in a kind of Orpheus and Eurydice situation, really trying hard to turn around and see that person there behind me but being unable to see them, having them obscured from me. Would I still be sent to the underworld for that failed attempt at real sight. I wondered that almost unconsciously, mythology wasn't the sort of thing I thought about at all.

I stood outside the station for a long time just prolonging the feeling of having said goodbye to Luke outside a train station. I did know that there would be a point in the future when I would look back on this afternoon and long for it, really long for the feeling of Luke sitting opposite me in some cafe and talking in a pointless and even hostile way about the internet and women and the dark. Many things to come would be worse than that terrible afternoon, many things in the future would be emptier and bleaker than that stupid afternoon.

○

I went for a walk over some fields in the night. I walked all the way to the motorway at the back of the fields, I guess it was a motorway I'd been driven along as I'd been taken to and from university in the past. I watched the cars just driving in a dimly lit red way along the motorway, endlessly driving even in the middle of this random night. The vague way that the cars were lit up by their tail lights reminded me of the light that comes from holding your finger up to a flashlight, the faint red glow which bleeds through skin. That light had always felt very illicit to me somehow, almost frighteningly sensual. It really wasn't right, for light to travel straight through someone's finger like that. I knew, though, as I stood there watching the cars, that in another reality it would have been beautiful to me, the idea of warm light seeping right through someone's finger, seeping through their tissue and their skin into the sky and the air. In another life that would have been mine, that warm wet dissolution of the boundaries of the body.

Once Anna's exams had finished we went for a walk. We sat on a bench by the river and talked about next year. Anna was anxious about a Master's degree she had applied to in Spain, Jacob had applied to a parallel Master's programme and been accepted and now everything was hanging on her own acceptance to the Master's programme, even the flat that she and Jacob were planning to rent was contingent upon that and then even once she was accepted she had to think about how to fund the cost of living, she would have to find some part-time job which would allow her to earn a passable amount of money while also completing her Master's degree. These problems did sound extremely stressful but somehow they also felt false to me, and distant, almost arbitrary. It was an insane thing to think, I knew that they were real problems with real material and emotional consequences, they were much more real problems than 'love' was. But Anna also felt that they were solvable, she said that despite these problems she was ready to get out, she was ready for some new thing to begin.

I didn't know what to say about graduating then. I told Anna that there was nothing I really wanted to do, which meant that the things I desperately did want were inaccessible to me and that thinking about some year in which I was living in some place and doing some job and continuing not to access those things was unbearable,

I would really rather die than live a cold empty year like that entirely alone in a flat somewhere. Anna said What do you think will happen with you and Luke and I could tell from the gentle way she said it that she knew Luke was the reason I was crying as I sat there on the bench saying there was nothing at all that I wanted. I suddenly wished that I had spoken to Anna about everything all along, I suddenly felt that things might have been different if I had spoken to Anna about them. But feeling that Anna understood me was very different to feeling that Luke understood me. It couldn't hold me, the fact that Anna might be able to understand things, it couldn't take me anywhere.

○

That week there was a sandstorm, some sand had blown across the ocean and invaded the sky so that it looked dim and orange like a dirty blanket. I walked around the city in that dirty blank light, I didn't see any sand grains, it seemed like the sand was more metaphorical. Everything looked strange to me, all the arrogant church towers and libraries, the shops, all of the nail salons and the fields even. None of those things felt like things which had been mine. They reminded me of a toy I'd had as a child, a View-Master, you looked through its eyepiece and saw a photo and if you pulled down on a lever then it would be pulled away into an unknown chamber in the View-Master and replaced with another. All of those photos were replaceable, none of them stayed mine and it felt like there wasn't any way back to them after I pressed down on the lever and removed them from the screen. I can't remember what the theme of my View-Master had been. I think it was cities, I think the View-Master had shown me photos of different European cities.

During that sandstorm the musician SOPHIE died, she died while standing on her balcony trying to take a photo of the moon. I had discovered SOPHIE through Luke's Spotify so many months ago, once I had sent him her song It's Okay to Cry and he had already known the song, he had already known it because I had found it through him. I bought a neon green candle for SOPHIE, I lit the candle and then realised I had nowhere to put it, I owned nothing that a candle could stand upright inside of. I just held the candle until it was half burnt out and then I blew it out completely. I was still thinking about SOPHIE, I was still thinking about that death, that death caused by a desperate attempt to capture something.

○

I had a dream about my life next year. In the dream I was a gallery assistant, I was standing around inside some art gallery. The exhibition I was attending was a lot of small piles of damp grey cloth. The piles were meant to represent something, I knew that in the dream, they were not inconsequential but still the exhibition felt pointless. When people asked me questions I had to say, I am a big fan but not an expert. Then I had to direct them to the expert, who was another gallery assistant.

After I woke up from that dream I fell asleep again almost immediately and had a second dream about videos of babies. In the dream I was in a lecture and being shown so many videos of babies, tiny wrinkled babies crawling across their mothers' stomachs to their breasts, so many babies performing this exact same action. The videos really upset me in the dream, even the old and unreadable videos which were so low resolution that the babies were just grey-and-white pixels moving slowly across space. In the dream I understood that the videos upset me so much because I knew something quite serious: that I was the baby and Luke was the mother, and the mother was withholding things I needed to survive. She was pulling very far away from my little wrinkled fingers as they reached out for her swollen breasts. It was an off-putting analogy, I wished my brain hadn't thought of it.

○

On Monday it was my graduation. This felt surreal to me and like something out of some stupid and irrelevant movie made by a man who was nostalgic for the fancy old rooms of university and all the other men there who he would talk to about philosophy and discover new fundamental physics concepts with. I actually felt quite angry to be graduating, I felt almost tearful with rage that whole day. I felt that graduation was supposed to mark some entry into the world but for me it had nothing to do with that. My entry into the world had been already barred, some harsh door already slammed somewhere, some passageway or tunnel already blocked off. My name was called out and I barely even registered it, it sounded like the name of just some woman, some other woman in the world living some alien life. I really hated the sound of my name read out like that.

○

I had to leave university then, I had to pack up my things and take the pictures off my pinboard. Those pictures were very depressing, somehow I had never realised that. There were so many photos I had taken as a child, bad photos of skies and rivers and brown ground. There was a photo of me standing in between my parents on our old street wearing an orange jumper that my grandmother had knitted for me. Seeing that photo made me feel very empty and mournful like my grandmother had died or like my parents had divorced but they hadn't. It was something else that had died, something else that had been killed, I understood it as I stared into my child self's wide face. There was a postcard of a truck moving sideways through great slashes of blue and orange light, a Jonathan Meades postcard, and another of his, a bright blue bench standing desolately beside the sea. There was a Yoshitomo Nara postcard which said OH! MY GOD! I MISS YOU. I took that postcard down last, I let it watch me take down all the others. Oh my god I miss you, it really was true. My pinboard was empty.

Anna got a call to say that she had been accepted into the Master's programme, she would go to Spain immediately and start living in the flat with Jacob. We constructed some situation in which I would go with them on the plane and stay for a couple of days as they moved in, I would see the city with them, I would watch them unpack their things. I bought my ticket online, I saw a Google advert for £8 tickets but actually the tickets were £216. There was nothing I was saving up for, this was indisputable so of course I bought the tickets. Wasting my money was a step towards obliteration which didn't involve my body, it was a completely immaterial step towards suicide and that was what I was looking for, immateriality.

It was confusing, packing up my room while simultaneously packing to go to Spain with Anna and Jacob. I ended up packing a very random bag to take to Spain, I packed pyjamas which was good but then also a book about how to interpret the deeper meanings which were present inside children's playing behaviour and a small purple vibrator. I hadn't remembered that I had a vibrator, I couldn't remember ever using it. At one point my own hands had been enough for me, I did remember that quite clearly. At one point my own body was enough.

○

We got a plane very late on Friday evening, it was after ten o'clock when we boarded and the lights stayed off for the whole flight as if the passengers were sleeping right there in their seats. I turned on the small light above my seat and read my book, it was *Flights* by Olga Tokarczuk. In the part I was reading some man was on an island and trying to find his lost wife and child, everyone on the island kept telling him that it was impossible for a person to get lost there, the island was too small and too isolated. Where was his wife? It seemed like she had run away from him, and he had no idea why she would do that. But the lost wife wasn't the point at all, she was barely even real. Really the novel was about motion and time and meaning and history, lots of the characters were historical, there was a seventeenth-century anatomist and a nineteenth-century pianist and the pianist was actually Chopin. I didn't understand how Olga Tokarczuk had done that, how she had constructed a novel which was so ambitious in scope that it wasn't about just some person at all, it was about concepts. If I wrote a novel it would be about some girl, she might think about motion and time and meaning but it would never extend beyond that, no one would ever say it was a novel about motion and time and meaning. It would be a completely unconceptual novel trapped inside the limited mind of some girl, I was sure of that.

When we landed we got onto a bus and drove through the night towards the city. I tried very hard not to speak to Anna and Jacob. I knew that they were experiencing something separate from me in that moment, they were experiencing the start of their lives. I was just seeing some more objects, some more roads and some more lights. I sat quietly on the bus, I looked out at the roads and at the lights as they passed me by and faded into darkness.

○

We spent a lot of that weekend inside Anna and Jacob's new flat. It was an unbelievable flat, the walls were stone but it didn't feel cold at all, it was extremely bright with huge windows looking out onto the roofs of other flats and a few very old domed buildings. Anna said the city was arranged in blocks, neatly divided into endless equal squares but it all looked random from the windows, roofs everywhere, I couldn't see the logic of the city at all. There was one building perfectly positioned in the centre of the view, a detached pale green building with a long strip of windows round its centre. It looked like something from a Wes Anderson movie, that pastel building standing alone there symmetrically positioned in the centre of my visual field. What a stupid thought to have about Barcelona, that it looked like a still from a Wes Anderson movie.

Anna and Jacob unpacked their things into the cupboards and drawers and I didn't really help because then they wouldn't know where their things were. They started setting up the Wi-Fi and then suddenly stopped, I guess they remembered I was there on my stupid immediate visit. I tried very hard to show that I didn't mind them being busy by occupying myself with things like writing detailed photographic descriptions of the view that I could see out of their windows. I had never been interested in descriptive writing but suddenly it seemed like the only type of writing imaginable, aimlessly describing things forever. There would always be endless things to describe. I didn't really feel any drive to leave the flat and that was very depressing. Places really meant nothing to me, movement really meant nothing.

○

In the evening we went for a drink in a courtyard in the city's 'gothic' quarter. We drank cheap beers and talked about writing. Jacob said he wanted to write more that year, he wanted to write a book about the conclusions he had come to during his degree. I thought it sounded great and I said that he should make it autofictional, it should be about not just his studies but also his own life and feelings but Anna and Jacob both agreed that it would never happen, Jacob would never write that book of conclusions, not in any genre. Anna said, then, that she didn't understand writing, she couldn't write in any kind of authentic voice, she just associated writing with writing stupid stories in high school, stories that began with sentences like The thunder clapped. Anna said, I still am that thunder clapped person. That was funny to me but also depressingly true. There were so many situations in which expression was so endlessly limited by form, Anna wasn't wrong about that.

We walked back to the flat then. Anna made us fried eggs on toast, she toasted the bread in the pan next to the eggs so that the bread was slightly fried in egg, it was implausibly delicious. I had the very clearly articulated thought that I didn't understand how this could be something Luke didn't want, us sitting next to one another on the sofa of some beautiful flat, slightly drunk off very cheap beers and eating little fried eggs on top of toast. Luke would have fitted into that situation perfectly, sitting beside me on the sofa as Anna and Jacob sat beside each other too and talked about the things that they would do that year, the ways that they would organise their time, the libraries they'd study in and the types of transport they would use to get there. Those things were much more for Luke than they were for me, beers, fried eggs, specific plans, sitting comfortably on a sofa with random TV playing quietly there in the background. Those things were not for me, those things were Luke's, he didn't want me to have them with him and so he didn't want me to have them at all. Luke knew I couldn't have those things without him, he knew I couldn't make them mine.

There was a spare room in the flat and I went in there as soon as I had that thought. The spare room led out onto a balcony, Anna and Jacob were really living in a flat with its own stone balcony. I sat there on the plastic chairs, looking out over the roofs of all those other endless flats. I was crying as I sat there with that stone barrier erected in front of me, standing between me and the great fall to the ground. I went back into the room then and slept very badly with all the lights still on.

○

The next day Anna took us to an old swimming pool outside the city. We sat on the bleachers looking out into the pool and over the city, and it really was an amazing sight, that bright blue pool and the city stretched out behind it and the sea there in the distance too, vaguely merging with the sky and also bright blue and illuminated. Beauty really did do something, beauty could stun you for a moment and I did find that compelling, sitting with Anna and Jacob looking out at that view in the bright sun. It didn't occur to me to take a photo, it felt to me in that moment that beauty was something which was nice but which didn't fundamentally mean anything, it couldn't sustain you and had nothing to give you. We walked down the hill then and it felt like something somebody would do when they had so much life ahead of them, when they were at the very beginning looking down across the sunlit wooded path. I imagined the feeling as I walked down the hill: standing there with something great really stretched out in front of me. I remembered Luke's freckled legs right then and skidded down the hill a bit, the gravel carving dents into the heels of my Nikes. Luke's freckled legs: the thought of them had made me fall. The memory of Luke's body, carving channels through the soles of my shoes.

○

My ticket back was to Luton, an airport I had barely even heard of, and I kept forgetting which airport I was meant to be going to and then where I was meant to be going from the airport, I really found it hard to remember whether I was going back to university or back home or somewhere else; that also felt plausible somehow, that I might be going to some other unspecified place. Then for no reason after I got off the plane I went into an airport Travelodge and booked myself in, it cost £78, and then I went into a Pret and bought an avocado and olive baguette and some vegetable crisps, some salt and vinegar crisps and something called a Love bar which was a sort of caramel-coated flapjack, and a kombucha, I didn't even know what that was and it didn't taste nice. I ate those things on the hotel bed beneath a red-and-blue photograph of a vague swirl and a slightly distorted photograph of a phone box. I didn't feel like reading my book, I just lay there on the bed and used up all my data watching different videos people had put onto Instagram. I couldn't really see what the videos were of somehow, there were people in the videos and places and objects too, there were lots of different things.

In the bathroom there were ants, a lot of little ants running around inside the bath. I tried to explore the question of whether it would feel good to kill them with water, it didn't feel good and I stopped. I hadn't expected that it would feel good, drowning those ants. They reminded me of Heigel's mice, tiny things moving around along endlessly predictable paths, trapped inside some great eternal cage.

I went back home then, I took three different trains the next morning. In the aisle of each train there was a cartoon video playing about what we should do in an emergency. In an emergency we should smash all of the windows and then jump out of the train onto the tracks.

When I got home all my plants had died. There were yellow bits of leaf breaking off everywhere and one little tree's stem had gone totally rotten and pliable, it was so easy to distort the stem now, to press it into new wrong twisted shapes. Had the plants been dying for a long time, had I somehow not noticed their gradual decline into death? These plants had been sitting on my desk and on my bookshelf and floor as me and Luke had eaten all those dinners in my room, as we had sat together in the dark. Now they were dead and I had no witnesses at all.

○

The differences between days became mostly about weather. Some days were sunny and I walked around the field behind the house, some weirdly long field which made my nose stream endless fluid. Then some days were rainy and I sat inside my room typing different pointless things into my laptop, or I would walk along the canal in the rain to some cafe and type things into my laptop from there. My body really did love inserting different memories of Luke into my laptop and for a while I thought that it might help me, to put those memories somewhere outside myself, but it obviously didn't help at all, the memories were not any less present in my mind after I had spat them out.

Really it was impossible to even breathe without thinking of Luke. My own breath reminded me of how I had at some point in the unreachable past breathed out into the same room into which he was breathing, our breath mixing in the air, the air made up of some complex molecular fusion of both of us. Did that air still exist somewhere out there in the world or had it separated, now, into its composite parts, just my breath and Luke's breath drifting around in the atmosphere, maybe hovering above some mountains somewhere or some ocean. The time two thirty reminded me of Luke. Every day at two thirty I was reminded of some joke Luke had made, he had asked me the time and I had said Two thirty and he had pretended to mishear me and to think I had exclaimed Tooth hurty! as if my tooth hurt so badly that it was impossible for me not to shout about it. Now if my tooth hurt there would be no one to tell. Every pain was some unspeakable pain.

The problem with my ears started again, again my ears were blocked and the world was inaudible. I know the moment it started, I was walking around a park circling some tiny lake, on wooden boardwalks, and listening to Two Weeks by FKA Twigs, to FKA Twigs singing You're the only one who resonates, all those throbbing gasps and supersaws, I turned the volume up as far as it could go and I could feel, then, a slight popping in my ears, the wet compression of some hot thing: my ears closed themselves. I kept listening to the song, I could still hear the sounds and words very faintly through my closed-up eardrums as I walked around the wet things in that park, the leaves and the patches of mud, all the wet flowers.

It was almost too metaphorical to take seriously, the return of this ear problem. At one point in the past the world had dulled itself to a loose background drone and Luke had been there to supplant it, he had been there to replace the world with his perceptions of it and that was perfect, that was all I ever wanted, me and Luke sharing a single channel of input like lab animals being exposed to the same stimuli as one another forever in order to probe loosely and pointlessly at vague questions of the environment and the brain and development and congruence. Now there were things I couldn't hear and there was nobody to hear them for me. I was unable to elevate myself above the limits of my bodily sensations.

○

I went to London to go look through museums. I went to Tate Modern. There was a looping video of lots of little insects carrying sequins in their tiny insect hands across some leaves and twigs. I watched that video for almost an hour and I didn't look at the notice even once, I really didn't want to know what some person thought the video was meant to be about. Then there was a video of scaffolding on a beach being dismantled and the static sea behind the scaffolding. I loved that video too, I watched the structure being broken apart until all that was left was the pale stones of the beach. I really felt in that moment that all art should be like those videos, pointless extended observations of real things that happened, real things that meant nothing except that they were things that could happen, some insects could walk, some structure could be effortlessly dismantled.

This art reminded me of a story Luke had told me about Mia. After they broke up he found out that she had started making some kind of woollen sculptures, balls of wool joined together with wire. When he heard this Luke was afraid he had somehow repressed Mia's creative urges, the fact that she had started making art just after they broke up really worried him. It made me nauseous to remember that anecdote, it made me nauseous with sadness. Despite all the things that had happened Luke still hated himself, he still felt he was some bad and harmful presence in the world. Why had my opinion been so inconsequential, why had it meant nothing that I really did love him and that he had made me almost entirely happy for a month or two of my senseless life. I don't know why those things hadn't mattered.

○

I bought some vaginal dilators from the internet to torture myself with. When I typed Vaginal dilators into Google lots of cow dilators came up, huge steel claws that you could shove inside a cow and expand so that the cow's vagina would be prised open. Those metal claws reminded me of an awful instrument I'd heard about, for making sausages: the instrument shot a cylindrical blade into the body of an animal, and the blade closed itself, and pulled out a sausage-shaped piece of meat. I think that was a real thing I'd read about somewhere.

The human dilators were just plastic rods, they had no moving parts. I lay down on my bed and pushed the dilators at my body. The biggest dilator was the size of my whole hand when I made a fist. I pushed that dilator at myself and it felt like my internal walls might split, that the muscles might tear, thick clotted blood spreading all over the plastic body of the stick. But when I looked down it was barely even touching me, its whole length was dry and clean, touched only by the air around it. Only its rounded end was damp. It was a new form of self-harm I had invented for myself: inflicting some sharp frightening pain upon the most interior muscles of my body.

○

Luke sent me a message, he really did, Luke messaged me on Facebook and I saw his name on the screen of my phone. It almost didn't matter what the message said, the experience of seeing his name there was so strange that it was a complete experience in itself. At some point in the past that had been normal to me, something not even worth thinking about, Luke's name carrying with it a message he had sent me because he wanted to tell me something, to take something out from his life and to give it to me.

When I opened this new message it was about his birthday party, the party would be in two days at his parents' house. After the message Luke had sent me an animated sticker of a tiny cartoon rabbit endlessly jumping up and down inside the wide-open hand of a person.

I had so many dreams about Luke's party that night, different possible endings throbbing through my brain like in one of those Choose your own adventure books where you could determine what the ending of the book would look like, inadvertently, through your own blind choices. I had a dream that Luke wasn't at his party, it was actually his sister's party and then I had a dream that Mia was at the party and Luke came to find me and to tell me about it, he was crying and I comforted him on the street outside his house. I had a dream where Luke pushed me up against some kind of stone fireplace and kissed me violently in front of everyone and I could feel his whole body through my body as he kissed me, I woke up wet. I had a dream that Luke's party was in a field and everyone was dancing in the field and looking up at the stars. There was a parachute like in primary school when the teachers had let us all play together underneath one. I had a dream that Luke gave me some bad ham pizza and the pizza was cold.

I knew when I woke up that whatever happened at the party, now my memory of it would be false and confused, filled with these meaningless things that had been born out of the inside of my mind. That was a very bad thought, all these fake things which were now a part of something real. Obviously Luke would never kiss me, obviously Luke would never even give me a bad piece of pizza.

○

On the first train to the party I started reading *My Year of Rest and Relaxation* which I had bought from Waterstones on the way to the station but I stopped reading it almost immediately: it was not the right book choice for that moment. *My Year of Rest and Relaxation* was about a nameless woman living some depressing awful year inside her flat, taking pills and drinking lots of creamy coffees which she bought from a bodega. She kept thinking about this man Trevor but Trevor never answered the phone when she called him. Really the nameless woman in *My Year of Rest and Relaxation* just wanted one thing which was to fade away from life, she just wanted to sleep forever. It really wasn't the right book to read on the train to Luke's party.

Instead I read lots of interviews with Ottessa Moshfegh about her experience of writing *My Year of Rest and Relaxation*. Ottessa Moshfegh said that the historical and geographical context of that book felt arbitrary to her, 9/11 happens in the book for example but it wasn't the point at all. Really it was a novel about what it is like to exist and to know that you can only be one person. That could happen anywhere at any time, that experience. She was right about that, situational details and objects and people were just random, like props to illustrate how it felt to be desperately alone inside your body and your mind and the world. That made me feel better.

○

I walked from the train station to Luke's parents' house, I walked alone along some route that Google recommended to me which was not one Luke and I had ever taken together, it was a new route through inexplicably busy streets filled with shops. And then the shops thinned out, I passed a huge and cuboid castle standing darkly on a hill against the sky. It was a long walk to Luke's house. It reminded me of some sentences we had been shown in school as examples of really good writing. One of the sentences was It was going to be a long cold walk, I thought as I looked up to the stars. Then another sentence was It was going to be a long cold night, I thought as I looked down to the sea. Somehow no one thought it mattered: that those two examples of great writing were identical. I realised then that obviously I couldn't have remembered those sentences from primary school, obviously I had invented that memory. Why had I invented that memory? Those were actually the things that I thought about, as I walked a long cold walk along the streets towards Luke's party.

Finally I arrived at the house, it was still light and I walked up the steps to the front door. I felt a sudden inexplicable wish for Luke's parents to be in; in that moment I felt that they might be able to understand the things that I was feeling, and feel pity and even love for me as they saw me standing out on the stone steps which led to their front door. They'd see me standing there, almost crying from the pain of my deathly unrequited love for their son. I really did feel that they might love me for that, that they might take me in their arms and tell me they wished that he had chosen me. Somehow that was a soothing thought: the great pity Luke's parents might feel if they saw me standing there outside their house as darkness fell and drowned everything all at once.

Luke answered the door then, he was wearing a blue knitted hat with a sort of cartoon monster on it. His body language, actually the whole atmosphere of him was unfamiliar, he seemed slightly languid and relaxed in some quite alien way like a person lying drunkenly on a picnic blanket in the sun. Luke said Oh hi and I said Luke hey happy birthday. They didn't look frightening, the things that passed between us, but we didn't hug then, Luke's body language signalling that I should walk past him into the hallway and I left my bag and coat there beside other people's things.

The house was very full, it turned out that lots of people had been at Luke's house that day already and that they had all gone to a park together and then to a bar. Somehow I worked these things out very quickly without anyone saying anything that was addressed to me. I didn't recognise anybody there and they looked slightly less specific than my mental image of Luke's friends, lots of the men just looked like standard men, some of them really built and muscular. There was generic music playing, generic 2000s pop music. I guess that was ironic somehow, that was ironic to somebody: the music that I'd heard inside of supermarkets, toy shops, dentists' waiting rooms when I had been a child and I didn't know what love was, what the music was about.

It was important to me to make it clear that I was younger than the other people at Luke's party, I said some stupid vapid thing about being unable to believe that Luke was twenty-four, that was so old, that was so shocking. I didn't even recognise my voice as I stood inside Luke's hallway surrounded by strangers and made pointless inane comments about him being older than me. It was just necessary to stress that I was in a completely different category to the other people at Luke's party, and that it was just because of my age. Because actually I was completely uncomparable with everyone else there at that party, I was some creature, I was Man-Bat there inside Luke's party. But it would have been impossible for me to explain why.

○

I stood around with a beer in my hand, I stood in Luke's living room and looked at old photos of him and his sisters. Luke had had long hair as a child too and a weird flat smile like a frog, obviously a smile he was doing very effortfully, really forcing his mouth into it. I felt an awful feeling building in my throat as I stood there seeing real evidence of Luke's self-consciousness even as a small, sweet child standing in big striped shorts and two T-shirts on top of each other beside his pre-teen sister. I stood there looking at that photo for a long time with the stinging feeling growing in my throat, some thirsty desolate feeling building there inside its pink walls. I didn't know if there were other people in the room with me, I didn't know if that ironic music was still playing, or maybe I did know but I wasn't conscious of those things, I was standing there in some impenetrable cage like in one of those plastic bubbles you could stand inside and roll around in.

Luke came over to me then and he said You know I can't be with you all evening. He didn't say it unkindly, he said it almost gently but still it felt like an awful thing to say to me as I stood there alone inside his living room. I had needed him to offer me everything he had and to give me his entire selfhood for hours and hours of course but I hadn't articulated that need, I hadn't asked for anything, I had never asked for anything, I had never in my life asked Luke for anything. I walked away from him without responding, my only response was that I was crying and I knew that Luke would think I was trying to make him feel bad but I really wasn't. My body was speaking in a language that was completely out of my control and that I could barely even read myself, my stupid body droning on and on forever. Luke hated me for that crying, I could feel that he hated me even as I walked away from him. I could feel his hatred emanating out from where he stood, I couldn't feel his presence or his eyes on me but still I could feel his cold hatred pressing into me. I walked away from that hatred towards nowhere, I walked towards a door which led me out of there.

○

I stood in the garden for a long time, in my T-shirt, holding nothing in my hands. I wasn't really watching or seeing anything but was at the same time very acutely aware of the feeling of standing entirely alone in Luke's parents' garden with a party going on ahead of me through glass. That feeling was very vivid to me, that was a feeling I would remember for a long time. The glass of the windows and the wood of the door felt very important to me in that moment: those things were metaphors for something. I could have written an essay about that, I could have written an essay about the discursive function of physical barriers in the frightening burning feeling that lived deep inside my love for Luke. I could have written a thousand pages about that.

Inside, Luke was drifting between rooms, pieces of his body coming in and out of my centre of vision, pieces of his selfhood shifting behind glass, his pale arms, his ironic yet gentle poise, his clumsy stumbling tallness, the clumsiness a contradictory expression of his great eternal gracefulness as he moved in and out of rooms, collapsing into gleaming beer bottles, leaning onto sofa arms and doorways. There were balloons and a man was pretending to be stuck in the balloons. I couldn't tell if people thought that joke was funny, that joke of being stuck in Luke's balloons.

I was crying still as I stood there by the window and it was hard to tell if people could see me. Somehow the windows felt false, they felt unidirectional or like some great projected screen on which I was watching an arbitrary person's fantasy of Luke moving around inside a house. Luke himself seemed simulated, like a version of Luke made inside of The Sims. I thought about that for a while, about Luke trapped inside of The Sims. I remembered that Sims could perform three actions at once: they could interact with an object, look at an object and talk to a different Sim. Those were the things that it was possible to do, those were the options. I stood there and watched Luke do those things, I stood there for a long time with tears running down my face and neck, stood in the middle of his father's vegetable patches, those vegetable patches which his father must have planted wearing gardening gloves one evening after work all bent over the soil with his house standing up there ahead of him, his kitchen ahead of him, the countertops lit up and shining in the kitchen light.

I could almost feel Luke's child self standing there beside me, Luke's quiet frightened child self with his freckles and his secret paintings, Luke's child self who would have hated this party and these adults, his child self so oppressed by a great fear of some inarticulable loss. This was the loss, the loss was mine, it was my loss Luke had feared, my own loss that he had felt there in his future. I had lost Luke, I knew that then, I was falling further and further away from him like his childhood flat smile, like the finger he had broken playing basketball, those two shattered bone ends which had fused themselves together in their hidden bed of blood. Luke was ready for the world, he was ready for his party, he was buried deep inside of it with me out here behind glass inside some soundless patch of garden above the pond into which children might fall.

A man was standing there behind me then and somehow he understood what was happening very clearly and was saying Don't mythologise him, don't mythologise him, he's just a guy and I was saying I love him, I really love him barely audibly but at the same time so incredibly loudly. In that moment it meant nothing that the man was standing there, it felt like I would have been saying that exact same sentence regardless of whether or not that man was standing there beside me and telling me about how Luke was just some man. My words were aimed at no one, there was no one left to aim any kind of speech act at. I could feel that the man was trying to keep me outside in the garden while keeping Luke there in the house but Luke was looking over then and seeing me, seeing me crying on my knees beside the vegetable patches, and he was turning away and walking out into some other room, some room which was invisible to me from where I was in the garden with not one single piece of Luke visible to me.

○

There was a way to leave without walking through the house, there was a way to move straight from the garden to the street, the street which belonged to no one. I threw up in the gutter and watched the contents of myself fall out of me into the metal hole and onto the ground that surrounded it. I can't remember if I walked or stood still in that moment, I can't remember how long I stood there and how long I was walking for. Somehow the image I kept seeing was that crowd of men dancing, men who were Luke's friends, Luke's brothers, some great brotherhood of men. I wasn't sure if that was something I had even seen but the image did feel real to me. I was thinking clearly in that moment, I was thinking as I pictured all those men that there was some very different way in which events could have played themselves out. There was an almost tangible past or a future in which I had been Luke's muscled, bare-chested friend, dancing and dancing in his house and surrounded by people who were like me and who knew me and could see me. I knew it in that moment: I could have been any one of those men, taking dripping wet beer bottles out from Luke's fridge and downing them there in the centre of some crowded room. I could almost feel the bottle cold in my hand, I could almost feel the way that I would start to dance, moving first my feet and then my arms, letting my arms slam down, slamming my arms down, showing, with my dance, the pain that I had the capacity to realise. In another life I could have caused somebody so much pain.

I walked, then, to the hill that I could see ahead of me against the sky. As I stood there looking out across the darkness I thought of the hill that Luke and I had rolled down together so many months ago. I remembered how desolate I'd felt, watching those videos of Luke rolling down the hill and away from me; how desolate I'd felt despite the fact that we had so many conversations left between us, so many embraces, so many moments in which Luke really did like me and felt real concern for the way that I felt. There was a time when he had hungered for me, when he had wanted to see me stretched out ahead of him as I, too, had wanted him right there in front of me for as long as I had eyes and could see things. Now there was nothing: now everything that had been mine had been destroyed. I tried to work out if I wanted to die. I really did feel that I wanted to die but it felt ridiculous to say it, no one could possibly have any sympathy for that, it was so melodramatic. But deep within the heart of my body I did feel that wish to die. I felt already very dead, I felt that some fundamental part of me was completely dead and would never return to me.

I wrote Luke a very long and unkind message then, as I stood there on the hill. I wrote that I loved him and that I hated him for not loving me back, that I considered his refusal to love me an act of great cowardice. I wrote that a person cannot live like that, so completely closed to the world and so full of walls, that any person so full of walls will be alone forever. I wrote, What if no one loves you like that again.

After I sent that message I realised very suddenly and sharply that a great violence had been building inside of me for months. My body was unbearably full of crashing dangerous life, a real destructive urge as if it was scanning its environment for something to maul and really destroy. That violence had been building as my body endured so many months in which nothing happened to it, in which it gave nothing and received nothing, and sat untouched, bled out for Luke in some private secret place without expression. Death had been coming, destruction had been coming, I had known it all along, I had never doubted the promise of eventual death.

It was impossible, there, on that hill, to identify any meaningful destructive act. I kicked a public bin, I kicked the ground and then I punched some heavy tree trunk but there was no release of energy, no catharsis, not even pain. I looked down at my hands which had formed fists to punch the deadened tree, I looked down at my hands using my phone's cold gleaming flashlight. My hands were untouched, they were unblemished. The only blemish was a stupid pink rash that my body had self-generated, a rash with no external cause at all, no connection to the world.

I knew then that there was no point acting on the environment, there was some urgent need to let the environment act on me, to render me its own dumb object. Implausibly there was a great black lake on top of the hill, some deep black lake beneath the sky. The lake looked like a dominating presence stretched out ahead of me and I started wading into it and felt the water saturate my trousers, I felt it saturate the nylon of my knickers and my body did become heavy then, my legs did deaden slightly as they stood there in the water. I lay down on my back and felt great shocks of cold pass through my spine, and I thought that I was coming close to some overwhelming and obliterating feeling, some final pain. But I was just cold and uncomfortable, I had to climb out eventually. I sat dripping by the lake and looked up to the sky. Nothing was visible up there, no clouds or stars, no moon. I sat there for hours, looking up at nothing.

Disclaimer: The publisher warrants that every effort has been made to seek and obtain permission from copyright holders to reprint these and other excerpts cited in this volume at time of publication. Any omissions will be rectified immediately upon written notification to Les Fugitives by the copyright holder or their representative.

Quotations from 'U.F.O. in Kushiro' by Haruki Murakami, *The New Yorker*, © Condé Nast. Reprinted with permission.

Lines from 'Light, clarity, avocado salad in the morning' and 'Having a Coke with You' from *Selected Poems* by Frank O'Hara, edited by Donald Allen, © Frank O'Hara (Carcanet Press, 2005). Reprinted with permission.

Lines from 'I Want You To Love Me' by Fiona Apple, from the album *Fetch the Bolt Cutters* (Epic Records, 2020).

Lines from 'Door' by Caroline Polachek, from the album *Pang* (Perpetual Novice, 2019).
Quotation from 'Two Weeks' by FKA Twigs, from the album *LP1* (Young Turks, 2014).

Lines from 'The Place Where He Inserted the Blade' by Black Country, New Road from the album *Ants from Up There* (Ninja Tune, 2022).

HARRIET ARMSTRONG was born and raised in Oxford. She has had short stories and one essay published in *Granta, Kismet, Cōnfingō Magazine, The Georgia Review*, the *Virginia Quarterly Review*, Giramondo's *HEAT* literary magazine and *Forever Magazine*. In Autumn 2024, aged twenty-four, she was a Resident at the Giancarlo DiTrapano Foundation for Literature and the Arts. She lives and works in London. *To Rest Our Minds and Bodies* is her first novel.

Published by Les Fugitives:
In 'the quick brown fox' collection:

Charlotte Beeston
The White Flower

Penelope Curtis
After Nora

Lauren Elkin
*No. 91/92: notes on
a Parisian commute*

Erica van Horn
We Still Have the Telephone

Olufemi Terry
Wilderness of Mirrors

Kyra Wilder
Gloss

In translation from French:

Catherine Axelrad
Célina
trans. Philip Terry

Jeanne Benameur
*The Child Who
A Grammar of the World*
trans. Bill Johnston

Yann Chateigné Tytelman
Blackout

Ananda Devi
*Eve out of Her Ruins
The Living Days*
trans. Jeffrey Zuckerman

Colette Fellous
This Tilting World
trans. Sophie Lewis

Jean Frémon
*Now, Now, Louison
Nativity*, trans. Cole Swensen
Portrait Tales, trans. John Taylor

Mireille Gansel
Translation as Transhumance
trans. Ros Schwartz

Maylis de Kerangal
Eastbound
trans. Jessica Moore

Julia Kerninon
A Respectable Occupation
trans. Ruth Diver

Camille Laurens
Little Dancer Aged Fourteen
trans. Willard Wood

Noémi Lefebvre
*Blue Self-Portrait
Poetics of Work*
trans. Sophie Lewis

Nathalie Léger
Suite for Barbara Loden
trans. Natasha Lehrer
Exposition
trans. Amanda DeMarco
The White Dress
trans. Natasha Lehrer

Emilienne Malfatto
May the Tigris Grieve for You
trans. Lorna Scott Fox

Lucie Paye
Absence
trans. Natasha Lehrer

Shumona Sinha
Down with the Poor!
trans. Teresa Lavender Fagan

Clara Schulmann
Chicanes, trans. Clem Clement,
Ruth Diver, Lauren Elkin, *et al.*

Anne Serre
The Governesses
The Fool and Other Moral Tales
trans. Mark Hutchinson

Sylvie Weil
Selfies
trans. Ros Schwartz

EU Authorised Representative: Easy Access
System Europe - Mustamäe tee 50, 10621 Tallinn, Estonia,
gpsr.requests@easproject.com • ISBN: 978-1-7397783-6-1